About the author

J. M. Robson has been writing novels for a number of years and this is the first of her work to be published. A lover of horror and mystery books, she spends her spare time reading and writing. She is currently working on a number of projects including the sequel to *Three Little Words*.

Robson lives in a small village on the outskirts of Dundee, Scotland. She is married, has one son, and two beautiful Grandchildren.

She supports a number of animal charities in the UK and abroad including "Help Bulgaria's Street Dogs and Cats" and "Pongo Vet – Muscat Romania" and spends time with her own rescue dogs, taking them for long works in the beautiful countryside of Scotland.

THREE LITTLE WORDS

J. M. Robson

THREE LITTLE WORDS

Vanguard Press

VANGUARD PAPERBACK

A CIP catalogue record for this title is
available from the British Library.

ISBN 978 178 465 214 2

Vanguard Press is an imprint of
Pegasus Elliot MacKenzie Publishers Ltd.
www.pegasuspublishers.com

First Published in 2017

Vanguard Press
Sheraton House Castle Park
Cambridge England

Printed & Bound in Great Britain

Thank you, Ryan and Fiona.

CHAPTER ONE

September 2013
Moreno Valley Community Hospital,
Moreno Valley, California

Lilly Anne Freemantle rode the elevator to the second floor of the hospital. She got out and walked the long, white corridor to one of the rooms at the end. She hated being here. She hated why she was here. The place reminded her of death and as she passed each room, she knew that behind each door someone was dying – just like James.

She was tired and feeling a little cranky. It had been a long day and she had come straight from work to visit James. She was still dressed in the black trouser suit and pale blue blouse she had chosen that morning. She wished she had been able to go home for a shower or at least had the time to freshen up, but visiting time started over an hour ago and she had promised James she would visit him every day. Now that promise was becoming hard to keep and she felt guilty for wishing that James would stop fighting and free her from this awful nightmare.

At the end of the corridor she stopped before a closed, white door and took a few moments to prepare herself. Finally she opened the door and entered the warm, dimly lit room. She quietly walked over to the sole bed that occupied the sparsely decorated space. A monitor with flashing lights stood next to the white-sheeted bed. Three drip bags with different coloured fluids hung on a long, slender, silver-coloured stand, which were fed intravenously into James's bruised, thin wrist.

Pulling a seat up beside James, Lilly Anne nervously leaned in to look at her husband. Secretly she hated the sight of him. He scared her and she couldn't believe that this grey-coloured, hairless, painfully thin, shell of a man was her husband. He used to be so handsome, so muscular. Now it was hard to remember him as he once was, before the leprous cancer had consumed his internal organs, killed off his immune system and sapped him of energy and life.

Lilly Anne Freemantle gently held her husband's lifeless cold hand. 'Please let go, honey,' she begged as tears spilled from her eyes and trickled down her cheeks on to the white linen, leaving wet spots where they landed.

'You don't have to fight any more.' She continued her pleading even though she knew he couldn't hear her.

She jumped as he groaned loudly, his grey sullen face contorted with pain.

'You have been so brave but I think you should rest now. I am so proud of you. You have tried so hard to beat this but we both know that you never will. It's time for you to give in for both of our sakes.' She wished he knew that watching him die was also slowly killing her.

Getting up from James's bedside she walked over to the window ledge and looked out of the window. It was a glorious evening. There wasn't a cloud in the sky and the sun was beginning to set. She opened the window, just slightly, as the heat in the room was too much for her but she knew that James's, thin, gaunt frame could no longer sustain any body heat so she would not keep it open very long.

James groaned again. This time more loudly. He sounded like he was in real pain as if the cocktail of painkillers that was being pumped into his body were no longer working.

Lilly Anne returned to the bed and pressed the alarm. Within seconds a nurse entered the room. It was the charge nurse, a familiar face, a friendly face.

'Is everything all right?' the nurse asked as she entered the room.

'He's in a lot of pain tonight,' Lilly Anne informed her. 'Is there anything you can do for him?'

'I'll get the doctor,' the nurse said. She smiled at Lilly Anne. 'You look dead on your feet tonight. Are you having trouble sleeping?'

She hadn't slept a whole night since James had been diagnosed with liver cancer. That had been just two months ago and right from the moment he had been given the devastating news, the prognosis hadn't been good.

They had taken the advice of the doctor and James had immediately begun an intensive course of chemotherapy that had claimed his beautiful blonde locks and the rest of his body hair.

'A bit,' she lied. She didn't want the nurse to be worried about her. James was the one that needed and deserved the attention. He was the one dying.

'Would you like a cup of coffee?' the nurse asked as she made her way out of the room to get the doctor.

'That would be nice,' Lilly Anne said, bravely putting on a smile as she sat down again beside James.

'Good evening, Lilly Anne,' the young, male doctor said as he entered the room. 'How is James doing tonight?' he asked as he picked up the chart hanging on the end of the bed.

Lilly Anne leaned forward to check her husband as the doctor continued to study the chart. She thought she had seen him move, but of course she was wrong.

'He seems to be in a lot of pain.'

The words were barely out of her mouth as James opened his eyes, making Lilly Anne jump back with fright, the legs of her chair scraped across the floor, making a loud screeching sound as she reeled back in disbelief.

'He's awake,' she said to the doctor, her voice barely a whisper. She got to her feet and nervously edged back to the side of the bed. 'James, can you hear me?'

She watched as James continued to stare up at the ceiling, his eyes never blinking as if he were in a trance.

'James, can you hear me?' she asked again as she leaned in closer, her legs now touching the side of the bed. She was so near to him, the closest she had been in a long time. His skin looked so grey and thin, his sullen eyes were edged with big black rings and his lips were so white.

'James?'

Suddenly James shot an arm up and caught Lilly Anne by the shoulder. She watched in horror as his head turned towards her, his eyes rolling. Drool was running out of his mouth and down the side of his face, making Lilly Anne feel nauseous. His ghastly pale face and collapsed cheeks contorted and twisted with pain making his appearance even more ghastly to look upon. She felt repulsed by his bony touch and wanted him to let go of her before she screamed.

Lilly Anne hadn't noticed the return of the nurse who was now standing beside her. She was equally amazed by the fact that James was awake when he was so heavily sedated.

‘He’s trying to communicate with you,’ the nurse said to her as the doctor joined them at the side of the bed. ‘Say something to him,’ she encouraged. ‘This may be the last chance you have to talk with him.’

That was easier said than done. What would she say? Chatting to James was the last thing on her mind. All she could think about was getting away from the bed. The horrific image of James staring at her with his lifeless eyes while he drooled uncontrollably was too surreal for her.

Noises started to come from James’s mouth. Bubbles formed on his lips as he tried to form words. He was trying to say something to Lilly Anne.

‘What’s he saying?’ Lilly Anne asked. ‘Can anyone understand him?’

‘I… love… you…’ The words had been hard to get out but they were understandable to all present. James was saying goodbye, telling Lilly Anne he loved her for one last time.

Lilly Anne looked at the nurse and the doctor. They were smiling. They thought she would be pleased but as she continued to stare at them, as fear and helplessness crept through her entire body, they soon began to realise that she was having trouble dealing with James’s unexpected awakening.

‘I… love… you…’ he said again, drooling uncontrollably. Repulsive, green, slimy saliva, dribbled down his lips making Lilly Anne’s stomach wrench.

‘I can’t deal with this,’ she said and pulled herself free from James before running from the room as fast as her feet could take her. She didn’t look back. She couldn’t. She couldn’t bear to look at James a moment longer. The sight of him was making her feel so sick that as she reached the quiet of the corridor, she nearly threw up all over the clean, white floor.

She leaned against the wall. Her legs were trembling, her stomach in knots, her eyes wet with tears. Closing her eyes she tried to wipe the awful image of James from her mind and replace it with an old memory, one from happier times when he was healthy and handsome.

'Are you all right, dear?' the nurse asked, her voice soft, gentle and soothing.

Lilly Anne opened her eyes and wiped away the tears with the back of her hand. 'I'm fine.' She tried to smile but failed miserably. 'I just wasn't expecting him to wake up. I didn't think he would be conscious ever again.'

'It's highly unusual,' the doctor told her as he joined them in the corridor, 'and I doubt very much that he will ever speak again. I've just checked him over and his heart is very weak. I think he doesn't have much time left.'

'You should go and see him,' the nurse coaxed her gently. 'This is probably the last chance you will have to say goodbye.'

'I don't know if I can go back in there,' Lilly Anne confessed as the tears started to flow freely. 'I don't think I can tell him what he wants to hear.'

'I know it's hard for you,' the nurse continued to sympathise, 'but do you want your last moments together to be like this? Wouldn't you rather have the chance to let him know how you feel about him before he dies?'

Lilly Anne knew she was right. She would never be able to live with herself if she didn't say goodbye, no matter how hard it was going to be.

‘Okay,’ she conceded and took a step back towards the room. She turned back and looked at the nurse and doctor. ‘Will you come with me?’

The nurse smiled. ‘Of course we will, dear.’

They entered the room again. Lilly Anne leading the way, her head bowed as she dragged her heels.

‘Jesus! What the…’

Lilly Anne instantly lifted her head. What was wrong with the young doctor? He sounded surprised, as if there was something really wrong. She looked at the bed. It was empty, the sheets pulled right back, the blankets lying in a heap on the floor.

Her eyes darted around the room as her breath quickened with fear and panic. She couldn’t believe it. How could James have got out of bed? Taking another few steps into the room, she stopped dead as she caught sight of her deathly sick husband.

He was standing not far from the window, facing the wall.

The doctor laid a hand on her shoulder, making her jump as he gently moved her aside to gain access to the room.

‘James,’ he said, nervousness evident in his voice.

James was swaying on his feet. He didn’t look very stable. His bed gown was open at the back. His white bony legs and bottom were fully exposed. He slowly turned his head to look at them. He was still drooling and the front of his gown was soaking wet.

‘Come back to bed,’ the doctor said, taking a step towards James.

James didn’t respond to his voice, instead he turned to look at Lilly Anne. His lifeless eyes chilled her to the bone and she took a step back. She was ready to run from the room again.

'You, you… don't love me,' he stuttered.

He turned back to the wall. It was as if he couldn't bear to look at her. It was as if she had broken his heart.

The doctor and nurse were speechless and they turned to Lilly Anne, wanting her help to get him back to bed. They needed her to reciprocate his love. They knew it was what he wanted to hear and probably the only way they would be able to calm him down and get him back to bed.

Lilly Anne opened her mouth to speak. She didn't want James to die like this but before she could utter a word something happened to James. His legs started to twitch, then his arms and then the rest of his body. He looked like he was having a seizure.

'Do something!' Lilly Anne shouted as she stumbled backwards on shaky legs, as she tried to get out of the way of the doctor and nurse. What was happening to him?

The nurse and doctor rushed forward just as James screamed.

Lilly Anne covered her ears. It was horrible. The blood-curdling, harrowing scream seemed to go on forever and the awful sound stopped the doctor and nurse in their tracks, they looked as petrified as Lilly Anne did.

'Make him stop!' Lilly Anne cried. 'Make him stop!'

James turned to look at her again. His mouth still wide open, as the screaming continued. Then he stopped. He closed his mouth and turned back to the wall.

The nurse and doctor looked at each other in total bewilderment but before they could make another move, James started to convulse again. This time the shaking was so intense that Lilly Anne was surprised that he was able to stay on his feet.

'Help me restrain him and get him back to bed,' the doctor said to the nurse as he took hold of one of James's flailing arms.

The nurse tried to get hold of the other one but James pushed her away. She reeled back on her heels as she nearly fell over. The powerful blow took her by surprise. He was very strong for someone so close to death.

A loud gurgling started to come from James's throat. He sounded as if he were about to be sick. He turned to look at the doctor. The young man instantly knew he should get out of the way, but he was too slow and James projectile vomited into his face. Red frothy liquid poured from his mouth like a crimson waterfall.

'It's blood!' the nurse yelled as the doctor let go of James.

His face was completely red and he wiped away the blood with his trembling hands. 'Go get help,' he ordered the nurse. 'I'll try and get James back to bed.'

Lilly Anne couldn't believe what she was seeing. She watched as James continued to vomit blood. It looked like he would never stop and the freshly painted white wall he was facing was soon stained bright red.

James took a step towards the wall and placed his hands on the large, wet, bloody mark. He started to smear his hands in the liquid. Lilly Anne turned to the doctor for help, but he was by the bed, picking up a blanket from the floor. He used it to wipe the blood from his face and eyes before dropping it back on the ground.

'What's he doing?' she whispered as the doctor caught sight of James.

The doctor's eyes widened with shock and concern, he was equally surprised by James's strange and alarming behaviour. 'I don't know,' he confessed as James stopped what he was doing and turned to look at them.

His eyes slowly moved from person to person. His gown was now bright red and dripping wet with blood. He was an awful sight. It was a macabre image that would haunt Lilly Anne for the rest of her life.

The doctor finally made a move again, just as James's eyes closed and he fell down. His white, skinny, hairless body lay in a heap on the blood-soaked floor.

The doctor walked over to James, he squatted down, trying not to get his light-coloured trousers covered in blood and felt for a pulse. He looked up at Lilly Anne, his face grave.

'I'm sorry but he's gone.'

Tears filled her eyes and she walked over to where he lay in a large pool of blood. She stopped inches from the red puddle and stared down at her dead husband. He looked more peaceful now, his face no longer etched in pain. She wanted to reach out and touch him, tell him that she was sorry.

'I do love you,' she whispered tearfully, as she took another step towards where James lay. As she did so James's mouth opened.

'Did you see that?' she asked the doctor.

The doctor didn't reply. He didn't have to. James's sudden and unexpected movement took him totally by surprise and he reeled back, his feet slipping on the now congealing blood, falling with a hard thump on to his bottom.

'What is it?' Lilly Anne whispered as her vocal cords constricted with fear. Something was coming out of James's mouth. It looked like smoke, dark grey smoke. It continued to billow out of his gaping mouth as the terrified doctor tried to get to his feet. He desperately tried to distance himself from the strange phenomenon.

Sensing someone behind her, Lilly Anne turned to see the nurse standing in the doorway. She had covered her mouth with one hand, obviously trying to stifle a cry of fear.

Lilly Anne turned again to look at her dead husband, just as the strange cloudy mass that had escaped from his body started to move towards the window. There was something sinister about it, something evil and she shivered uncontrollably as panic and fear gripped her entire body. Then just as quickly as the apparition had appeared, the dark cloud was gone as it escaped through the open window and disappeared into the evening.

For a few moments nobody moved or said anything. They were all as equally stunned and shocked by what they had witnessed.

'Can you bring something to cover my husband?' Lilly Anne asked breaking the silence as she turned to the nurse.

The nurse didn't respond. She didn't even look at Lilly Anne. She was staring straight ahead. Looking at the blood-drenched wall.

Lilly Anne was afraid to turn back and look in the same direction as the nurse. She was afraid that the ghostly presence had returned. Slowly, she turned to look at the wall and instantly wished she never had.

James had left her a message, a bloody message that would haunt her for the rest of her life. With his last breath, his last ounce of energy, he had wanted her to know how he felt about her rejecting his love.

Bursting into tears, Lilly Anne wept uncontrollably as her legs gave way. The nurse rushed forward, steadying her and stopping her from falling over.

‘He didn’t mean it,’ she tried to reassure Lilly Anne as she helped her over to a chair.

Unable to take her eyes from the wall, Lilly Anne continued to cry as she read the large, blood-red words over and over again. James had crudely written just three words that were meant for her. Her rejection of his love had broken James’s heart and he wanted her to know that he no longer cared for her in the cruellest and most horrible way imaginable. The message he had left was simple but straight to the point.

‘DIE BITCH DIE’

CHAPTER TWO

October 2013
Perris, California

Juliet Petrie stood at the kitchen window. She was watching her four-year-old son Lennox happily playing in the backyard. He didn't even notice her checking on him. He was too engrossed digging away in the sandbox. He was busy at work with his bucket and spade, building up castles and knocking them back down again.

Taking a bottle of red wine from the unit under the sink, she unscrewed the lid. She knew there was nothing sadder than a glass of wine alone, especially at ten in the morning, but she really needed a drink. Pouring a hearty glass of the red liquid she gulped down the entire contents in one big swig.

Placing the bottle on the kitchen table she pulled out a chair and sat down before pouring another glass. A few seconds later the glass was empty again and she was ready for another refill. After six or seven glasses she would be back to her happy and carefree self. The way she had been before her husband had walked out on her.

It had been six months since Theo left her. He had run off with his young, blonde, sexy secretary. There had been no warning signs, no indications that he was unhappy with her and little Lennox, so when he called from the other side of the world to explain that he wasn't coming back, Juliet had thought he was joking. Days later the reality had hit her hard and now six months on, with bills piling up, she was finding it hard to cope with life as a single parent.

She knew that she had to find a job, but she didn't think her nerves could handle interviews and rejections. It had been more than ten years since she had worked. Theo had forced her to leave her job when they had married. He wanted her to be at home, to be the housewife. He liked to come home from work and find his dinner on the table, the house spick and span and his shirt pressed ready for work the next day.

At first she had missed the hectic office but after a few months of homemaking she started to enjoy being a housewife and loved making her husband happy. She thought she had a perfect marriage and when she fell pregnant and gave birth to Lennox she felt as if her life was complete.

She never once thought that Theo had stopped loving her. She had been careful about keeping her figure and at the age of thirty-nine years she still thought of herself as an attractive woman. Slender, pretty and tall, she always wore her long auburn hair in a well-groomed ponytail and her make-up was always immaculate.

Pouring another glass of wine she got to her feet again and made her way to the back door. She had better keep an eye on Lennox. A few days ago her elderly neighbour had found him out in the street. Juliet had been sure that she had securely fastened the latch on the gate but somehow Lennox had managed to open it and had escaped out on to the busy sidewalk.

Juliet shuddered as she thought about what could have happened to her precious son. If Mrs Anderson hadn't seen him he could have wandered out into the road.

Taking a large mouthful of wine she swallowed it hard. She couldn't bear the thought of losing her son. Lennox was all she had left and she closed her eyes as she removed the awful thought from her mind.

She wiped her wet lips and then headed back to her son. 'Lennox, honey, would you like some lemonade?' she called out as she opened the back door.

She felt the panic rise in her at the sight of the empty sandbox.

'Lennox, where are you!' she shouted as she raced into the garden, dropping the wine glass as she ran. The sound of breaking glass didn't even register as she caught sight of the open gate.

'Lennox!' She shouted louder as she dashed through the gate into the busy street. Her mind was racing and her heart was pounding so hard that she could feel her rhythmic pulse quickening as rapidly as her fears and worries for her beloved son.

She stopped dead on the sidewalk just inches from where Lennox was standing. He was perched right on the edge of the curb. Cars, trucks and trailers were closely whizzing by him at high speed. He hadn't even heard her calling out to him. She didn't have to see his face to know that he would be thrilled and excited by the noises and movement of the heavy traffic.

Juliet slowly sneaked up on her son. She didn't want to call out to him again as he might be startled and end up falling in front of a fast-moving car. She quickly grasped hold of one of his shoulders and yanked him back from the roadside.

'Mommy!' Lennox squealed out in surprise as she turned him to face her.

'What have I told you about leaving the garden!' she screeched at him. She was so angry but relieved at the same time. She didn't know whether she wanted to slap or hug him.

'I only wanted to see the cars,' Lennox said as his big, baby-blue eyes started to fill with tears.

'Do you know how dangerous it is out here? If you wanted to see the cars, you should have come and asked me. You know you are not to go outside the garden on your own.'

'I'm sorry, Mommy,' he cried. His chubby cheeks now wet from the waterfall of tears.

'Sorry isn't good enough. You promised me you wouldn't go out into the street again and the first minute my back is turned I find you out here.'

Juliet was livid and she walked quickly, as she practically dragged her upset son back to the house. She hoped none of her neighbours had seen him escape again. She was scared that someone might report her to social services.

Closing the gate behind her, she checked that the latch was securely fastened before leading her son back to the sandpit.

'I don't want you moving from here again,' she scolded him.

'I won't, Mommy. I promise,' Lennox cried as he sat down on the sand, his sweet, innocent face staring up at her. 'I love you, Mommy.'

Juliet was still angry. She needed another glass of wine. 'If you really loved me you wouldn't have left the garden.' She headed back to the house stopping briefly to pick up the pieces of broken glass. She threw the glass into the bin under the kitchen counter as she started to calm down.

She didn't like scolding her son but she didn't want him to grow up thinking that there were no consequences for wrongdoing. Picking up the bottle of wine she selected another glass from the sink and poured a fresh glass.

She could see Lennox sitting in the sandbox. He was still crying and was very upset. He was using the back of his hands to wipe away the tears that were still steadily flowing. Dirt, sand and snot were stuck to his cheeks, he looked really pitiful and the sight of him so sad and upset, made Juliet feel guilty.

Leaving the wine, Juliet made her way back out into the garden. Maybe she had overreacted but at the time she thought that Lennox could have been harmed or even killed by one of the passing vehicles. A thought that made her shiver, she really couldn't bear the thought of something bad happening to her baby boy.

'I'm sorry, son. I shouldn't have shouted at you like that,' she said stepping out of the doorway. 'Mommy loves you too,' she continued as she made her way to where her son was sitting. She was smiling now, hoping Lennox would forgive her for being so hard on him.

A high-pitched scream made her blood turn cold. The sudden, horrific sound had also frightened Lennox who had jumped to his feet and was now quickly running towards his mother. The noise had come from the sandpit, just yards from where Lennox had been sitting.

'What in God's name was that?' she half whispered to herself. She had never heard anything like that in her life. Had she drunk so much that her senses were so impaired that she was hearing things?

'Mommy, I'm scared,' Lennox said as he grabbed his mother round the legs and hid his face in her skirt.

'It's okay, darling. I won't let anything hurt you,' she replied as she gently ran a hand through his dark curly locks. She was trying to act brave, in a bid to calm her son, but she too was scared. What had made that awful sound? It didn't sound right, it didn't sound human, and whatever had made it was in her back garden.

She watched in disbelief as a ghostly figure rose from the sandpit, just inches from where Lennox had been sitting moments earlier. The apparition's long arms were outstretched and reaching out towards her precious son, as if it were trying to grab him, hurt him. Wispy, grey smoke billowed around the unearthly shape, making it hard for her to be sure of exactly what was standing before her. For that Juliet was thankful.

'What are you? What do you want?' she shouted at the creature, trying to be brave. She couldn't see a face. There was no real form, it was just a strange, billowing mass with arms, arms that were trying to take her son. She could feel it was evil, could sense it and she took a step back as she tried to distance her little boy from whatever was preying on him.

The unwanted visitor shrieked again. 'He was mine! He was mine!' It spoke as it floated towards Lennox.

'Get away from us!' Juliet shouted back. 'Leave my son alone. In the name of God leave us alone!' She wasn't a religious woman and hadn't been to church for a long time but she hoped God was listening to her now and would do all in his power to keep her son safe.

'Next time you won't be so lucky,' the evil apparition hissed in a wicked voice.

'You'll never take my baby from me!' Juliet retaliated as she got to her knees and protectively closed her arms around her son. 'Go away!' she shouted before she closed her eyes and started praying out loud begging God for his help.

'I will be back for him. Nobody escapes from me,' the ghostly figure hissed as it finally vanished.

Juliet opened her eyes. Relief replaced terror when she realised that her unwelcome, evil visitor had vanished.

'I promise I will always be good, Mommy,' Lennox whimpered as he continued to grip her tightly. 'Please don't let the monster get me.'

'Nothing is ever going to hurt you, my darling. Mommy loves you lots and lots and I will always keep you safe,' she said before kissing him on the top of his head.

'Can we go inside now?' Lennox asked as Juliet got to her feet. 'I don't want to stay out here,' he continued, fear evident in his small voice.

'Let's go, honey.' Juliet smiled down at him. She wondered how traumatised Lennox would be from the events they had just witnessed. 'I will get us both a big glass of lemonade.'

Her mind was still reeling from what had just happened. Something evil had nearly taken her son. If she hadn't gone outside when she did goodness knows what might have happened.

'Mommy, why did the monster go away?' Lennox asked as they entered the kitchen.

'I scared it away, honey,' Juliet lied. She was also unsure as to why the creature had fled. A lot of questions were going around and around her head. Where had it come from? What made it come after her son? What in God's name was it?

'Do you think it will come back for me?'

Juliet locked the door and turned to face her son who was now sitting on a chair at the kitchen table. He looked so small and delicate, his short legs dangling over the side of the seat.

Juliet got on to her knees and took hold of her son's hands. She stared into his big, blue eyes that were still full of tears and fear. 'I know it won't come back,' she said trying to reassure him.

'Do you think we should tell the police? Just in case it does come back and tries to take me away,' he asked.

'No, darling, I don't think we should tell anyone about what we just saw and I promise you that the monster will never ever bother us again.'

Juliet knew that it would be stupid to report what happened to anyone. Who would believe their story? After all, she had been heavily drinking all morning. The police would think she was nothing more than a mentally disturbed drunk and Lennox would be taken away from her and placed in care.

'But the police could come and protect us with their big guns,' Lennox continued.

'We don't need protecting, honey.' She gently stroked one of his cheeks. 'I know the monster won't come back.'

'If you are sure, Mommy.'

'I'm sure, baby.' Juliet smiled.

She got to her feet and took a large pitcher of home-made lemonade from the fridge. 'Go and wash your face and hands while I get your drink and cookie ready.'

She watched as Lennox gingerly got up from his chair and made his way to the bathroom. She had to make him go on his own. She had to make him think that everything was all right and that he was safe in the house.

She poured her son a large glass of cold lemonade and placed the cookie jar beside the drink. He could have as many cookies as he liked. Maybe it would help take his mind off what had just happened and also make him smile again.

She waited until Lennox was completely out of sight before she dropped into a chair. She was at breaking point. Her hands were shaking and she had to fight back the tears. She was worried, actually frightened and she knew that there was nothing she would be able to do if the evil creature did return for Lennox and she cursed her husband, the man that had abandoned them.

Who could she turn to for help, who could she trust and how did she defend her son from an evil spirit? She felt so alone, vulnerable, weak and pathetic, and for the first time since Lennox was born she wondered if she was a good mum because she knew if the spirit returned that she would be incapable of keeping him safe.

Hearing the bathroom door open she wiped away the tears that she could not hold back and tried to compose herself before Lennox came back. Getting to her feet she picked up the full wine glass and the wine bottle. She emptied the contents of both into the sink. At least there was one thing she was certain of, there would be no more drinking from today.

CHAPTER THREE

February 2014
Santa Clarita, California

Patrick Edwards got out of bed and wrapped a black, silk kimono around his sweaty, naked body.

'Not in the mood for seconds?' Simon Granger huskily asked as he lay between the rumpled sheets.

It was a very tempting offer but one that Patrick would have to refuse.

'Simon, we have to talk. I think you should get dressed,' he said as he pushed a hand through his damp, dark, tousled hair.

'Sounds serious,' Simon joked as he got up.

Patrick took a seat in one of the leather chairs by the double doors that led to the first-floor balcony. The doors were open and he could see down into the moonlit swimming pool below.

He watched as Simon wandered around the bedroom searching for his scattered clothes that had been discarded during the wild lovemaking. He was a very sexy man and Patrick had wanted him right from their first encounter.

Simon had been sent to Patrick's photography studio by one of LA's top modelling agencies. Patrick had enjoyed working with him as his muscular-toned body, handsome, youthful features and well-groomed golden locks made him very photogenic.

After a few sittings it became evident that the attraction was not one-sided. That hadn't surprised Patrick. He had always found it easy to get laid. His rugged, strong, manly frame and dark olive skin turned many a man's head. Yet he knew his hypnotic blue eyes and pert, tight ass were what made him especially sexually attractive.

After a long and strenuous photo shoot, Patrick had invited Simon out for a drink and before he knew it, one thing had led to another and Simon had ended up spending the night at Patrick's condo.

Patrick lit two cigarettes and passed one to the fully clothed Simon who was now dressed in designer black jeans, sneakers and a red fitted T-shirt.

'So what do you want to talk about?' he asked before taking a long draw on the cigarette.

'You know I am very fond of you,' Patrick continued as he leant back in the seat and crossed his legs allowing the gown to gape open revealing his athletic thighs.

'I should hope so. You know I could have you arrested for what you just did to me,' Simon joked. It was obvious he was a bit anxious. He always made stupid jokes when he was nervous.

'But I don't think we should see each other again,' Patrick continued.

'Are you breaking up with me?' Simon asked with disbelief in his voice.

'I'm sorry, Simon, but I just don't think we have anything in common.'

'Nothing in common!' Simon barked back at him. His eyes were ablaze with fury at the thought of being dumped. 'So I take it you were faking it earlier.'

'I wasn't talking about the sex.' Patrick got up from his seat and stubbed out his cigarette in the ashtray on the bedside cabinet. 'The sex has been fantastic. Mind-blowing in fact, but that is about it. We really don't have anything in common. We have different tastes in music and we have different friends. Hell! We even vote for different parties.'

Patrick knew that he was hurting Simon. He was thirteen years younger than Patrick and at the tender age of twenty still had a lot to learn about relationships. The huge age gap was one of the major factors why Patrick didn't see any future with him.

'You should be with someone younger, someone about the same age, who shares the same interests,' he said in a much gentler tone.

'But I don't want to see anyone else. I want to be with you,' Simon replied, his big brown eyes now filling with tears.

'I'm sorry, Simon, but it just won't work. I think you should go now.' He watched as tears spilled from Simon's eyes and ran down his cheeks.

'I love you, Patrick. I don't want this to end. Please give me a second chance. I can change.' He made his way towards Patrick with his arms outstretched. 'Please don't do this,' he begged and pleaded. 'I really am in love with you.'

Patrick took hold of his hands and stopped Simon from embracing him. 'You don't mean that. We have only been seeing each other a few months. You're getting love mixed up with lust.'

'I do mean it. Don't tell me how I feel,' Simon snapped at him as he released his hands from Patrick's grasp. 'So I take it you don't love me.'

The tears were now running off his chin and left dark, wet spots where they landed on his bright red top.

Patrick slowly shook his head. 'I'm sorry. No I don't feel that way about you.' He was starting to feel sorry for Simon, even a bit guilty. He wished now he had broken up with him over the phone.

'Please don't end this. I need you. I don't think I could live without you,' Simon continued his pleading, his red, wet, swollen eyes now full of pain and sorrow. 'I will die of a broken heart.'

'Don't say stupid things like that, Simon.' Patrick was starting to feel annoyed. 'Stop being such a drama queen.' Any self-respecting man would have left by now.

Patrick sighed, he was not sure of how to deal with Simon. 'You are a very handsome young man. I have no doubt that one day soon you will meet the right man and then you will realise that this has been the right decision for the both of us.'

'I don't think so. You will never know just how much you mean to me,' Simon replied, the bitterness evident in his voice.

The pair stood for a few moments in awkward silence. Patrick could tell that Simon had more to say but he didn't want to hear any more of his snivelling.

'Look, I will go and make us a drink.' He placed his hands on Simon's wet, red, puffy cheeks and tried to wipe away the steady flow of tears. 'You look like you could do with one.'

Leaving Simon in the bedroom, Patrick made his way down the stairs to the kitchen. He switched the light on as he entered the large, white room that was surrounded by new, immaculately clean, aluminium kitchen units and appliances.

How could he have been so stupid? He should have ended the relationship when he first had doubts, but as usual he had been thinking with his dick. He should have known better than to get involved with someone so young, from now on he would stick to men of his own age.

He selected two crystal goblets and a bottle of vodka from one of the cabinets before opening the freezer to search for some ice. He really was looking forward to this drink.

Placing a piece of ice in each glass, he then added a large measure of vodka to one of them. Raising the glass to his lips he quickly gulped down the liquid. The alcohol made a warm trail from his mouth right down to his stomach, instantly soothing him inside. The calming effect gave him a second wind and he felt strong enough to handle Simon's wailing and whining.

He refilled his glass and then added a small measure of the alcohol to the second. He didn't want Simon to spend a long time consuming the drink. Once he had finished Patrick would call a cab and get rid of him.

Carrying the two glasses he made his way back up to the bedroom. Taking a deep breath he entered the room. 'I know you're too young to be drinking but I thought this might help calm you down a bit.'

He stopped just inside the doorway. There was no sign of Simon. Taking a quick glance around the room he noticed that the en-suite bathroom door was closed.

'Are you in the bathroom, Simon?' he called out as he placed the glasses on the bedside cabinet.

There was no answer and Patrick wondered if Simon had slipped out while he was preparing the drinks, but he doubted it.

Patrick made his way to the closed door and gently knocked on it. 'Simon, are you in there?'

There was still no reply.

He was starting to feel annoyed again. If Simon thought that hiding in the bathroom would mean that Patrick wouldn't be able to throw him out, he could think again. 'Come on, Simon. If you are in there, you will have to come out sooner or later and face me.'

When again there was no reply, Patrick turned the door handle and was surprised when the door opened. He put his head round the door. 'Come and get your drink. The ice will be…'

He stopped short when he realised that Simon wasn't there.

'Where the hell are you, Simon?' Patrick called out angrily. Simon was starting to piss him off. 'Why are you hiding from me? The way you are behaving will not stop me from ending our relationship.'

A strong breeze was picking up outside and the white, sheer curtains of the patio doors were being tossed in every direction. Patrick made his way to the doors and tried to close them without catching the flimsy material.

Out of the corner of his eye, something attracted his attention. A blue shape was bobbing up and down in the pool below. Patrick couldn't tell what it was and edged out on to the balcony to get a better look.

He gripped hold of the balcony railing as he looked down in horror at Simon's lifeless body. He was face down in the water. His whole head immersed.

'Simon!' Patrick shouted as he ran from the balcony and back down the stairs. Simon couldn't swim. Surely he hadn't tried to end his life?

Patrick quickly opened the back door and ran out to the poolside. Getting to his knees he reached out and grabbed hold of Simon's body by one of his lifeless, outstretched hands. His skin felt cold and his fingers didn't respond to Patrick's touch.

Simon's head flopped forward as Patrick pulled him from the water and laid him beside the pool. He looked down at Simon's ashen face as he felt for a pulse. There was nothing.

Patrick started to panic. He didn't know what to do or how to resuscitate someone. He would have to call for an ambulance and he would have to be quick about it.

Getting to his feet he raced back indoors and picked up the phone. With shaking hands he dialled emergency services and was relieved that he did not have to wait for a response from the other end.

'Hello. I need medical assistance immediately. My friend, I think he's dead,' Patrick blurted out. He was breathless and speaking very fast.

'Calm down, sir,' a woman's voice replied at the other end. 'Take a deep breath and tell me your name and address and then what happened.'

Patrick managed to pass on all the required details. 'Please hurry,' he pleaded before putting down the phone.

Numbly he made his way back to where Simon lay. He hoped and prayed that the paramedics would be there soon and that Simon could be saved. He wouldn't be able to live with himself if he didn't make it. He had rejected Simon's love and now he might have to live with the consequences for the rest of his life.

He stopped dead in his tracks just feet from Simon's body. Was he seeing things or did the fingers on Simon's left hand just twitch? He instinctively took a step back as Simon's torso violently shuddered. Then his body was still again. Nervously he took a step towards Simon. Was he still alive?

Again without warning Simon's body started to shake, this time even more vigorously that his arm knocked against one of the poolside tables, knocking an ashtray to the ground.

The sound of breaking glass did not even register. Patrick's full attention was focused on Simon. He looked like he was having a fit. What the hell was going on?

Just as Patrick thought things couldn't get any more bizarre, Simon's mouth flew open. Frozen to the spot, Patrick prayed that Simon would take a breath. Maybe he was returning from the dead, maybe everything was going to be okay.

But Patrick's hopes were short-lived and he watched in terror as a grey, swirling mist escaped from Simon's wide gaping mouth. The dark, shadowy shape hovered above Simon's body furiously swirling and swooping as if it was about to attack.

Patrick cowered in fear as the strange phenomenon turned its attention from Simon and made its way towards him. He could feel his body tremble as the darkness moved closer and closer to him. He stumbled backwards into a poolside table and reached out to grab it before it fell over. He picked up the table and held it in front of himself in a bid to distance himself from whatever was about to attack him.

'You didn't love me. You didn't love me,' an icy voice whispered.

Patrick looked around for someone, was there someone else out here who had witnessed what had happened?

The voice spoke again and panic filled Patrick's lungs, making it hard for him to breathe normally, as he realised that the voice had come from the mist.

'Simon, is that you?' Was it Simon's tortured soul that he was seeing and hearing? Surely it couldn't be. There was something nasty and vindictive about the voice and he felt as if he was surrounded by an evil presence that was taunting him, enjoying watching his pain and guilt.

Patrick shivered. It was so cold and he felt chilled to the bone, he felt faint with fear and he swayed unsteadily on his feet..

Patrick dropped the table as he shivered uncontrollably and tried to pull the thin, silky robe, the only garment he wore, tighter round his quivering body.

'You did this to me. I told you I couldn't live without you. You killed me,' the voice continued.

It was Simon. It had to be Simon. He had come back from beyond the grave to punish him, maybe even hurt him.

'I'm so sorry, Simon. I didn't believe that you loved me. Please forgive me. Please don't hurt me,' Patrick begged as he dropped to his knees. He was crying now and scared, frightened out of his wits.

The apparition was now in front of his face but Patrick was afraid to look at it, afraid to look into it for fear that he might get a glimpse of Simon as he reached out of the darkness and grabbed him. Patrick closed his eyes. He was sure he was going to die and he could hear himself whispering for mercy as he waited for the attack to begin.

In the distance the sound of wailing sirens got louder and louder. The medical team he had requested were very close.

Patrick opened his eyes again, still expecting to be face-to-face with the ghost of Simon but now there was nothing there.

As relief engulfed his entire, quivering body, the emergency response vehicles screeched to a halt outside somewhere close by. Summing up the last of his energy, he crawled over to where Simon's cold, wet, body lay.

'I'm so sorry. Please forgive me.' He uncontrollably wept as he cuddled Simon's corpse.

CHAPTER FOUR

March 2014
Moreno Valley, California

'No. Please don't go. Please come back. Of course I love you,' Lilly Anne cried out in the dead of night.

Waking up from the awful nightmare she sat up in bed switching on the bedside lamp. Her face and neck were covered with sweat and her eyes were full of tears. She had been having awful nightmares ever since James had passed away.

The dream was always the same. She would find herself surrounded by darkness, in what felt like a large, empty room. Somewhere in the darkness James was watching her. She could hear him breathing, taking short, laboured breaths and the sound took her back to the day he had died. She would call out to him, she would apologise to him over and over again, tell him she loved him with all her heart, but her words always fell on deaf ears and she could sense him walking away, leaving her behind with her guilt as she cried out for his forgiveness.

Pushing back the quilt she got out of bed. Wrapping a red, cotton dressing gown round her body she made her way to the bathroom. Switching on the light she slowly made her way to the sink and turned on the cold tap. She dropped a clean, white flannel into the half-full sink and waited until it was soaked through before wringing it out. She pressed the wet cloth on to her sweaty forehead. The coldness of the cloth instantly soothed her.

How old she looked, she thought to herself as she stared into the bathroom mirror at her reflection. Her emerald-green eyes no longer sparkled with life. Her complexion was now dull and her once-vibrant jet-black hair hung lifelessly around her face.

The way her husband had passed away would haunt her for the rest of her life. She would never be able to live with herself for allowing him to leave this world not knowing how much she loved him.

Instead of returning to the bedroom she made her way downstairs to the study. It was only two in the morning but she knew there was no way she would get back to sleep again – not for a while anyway. Once she had dreamt and relived the events of that terrible evening all hopes of a decent night's rest were banished.

Her therapist had told her that the dreams were only temporary and once she had got over her guilt and was finally able to move on with life, they would vanish forever. That had been months ago and if anything, Lilly Anne was sure that the dreams were getting worse.

She made her way into the spacious study. The room had been James's favourite and he had chosen the decoration and oak furniture. Pictures of the New York Yankees hung on the walls and his sports medals and trophies lined the shelves and cabinets.

Taking a seat behind the desk, she booted up the computer, as she thought about the strange apparition that had appeared moments after James had passed away. No one had been able to give her a logical explanation for what she had seen and the doctor and nurse had both denied seeing the creature leave her husband's body. They had claimed that she had been distraught, upset at what her husband had written on the wall and that she had imagined the whole thing.

Beginning to give in to scepticism, she had started to believe that the stress of her husband's illness and the peculiar events leading to his death had brought on a hallucination. That was until she decided to do her own research. From websites and Internet chat rooms she had contacted other people who had encountered the supernatural phenomenon and a number of these people actually resided in California.

Through vampire, demon, mythology and other bizarre chat rooms she had communicated with numerous people who had also lost loved ones in bizarre circumstances. These were not the usual kind of websites that she browsed. Until recently she had only used the web a handful of times when she had been doing her Christmas shopping.

Of course some of the people she had chatted with had turned out to be cranks or people who idolised the Devil. Some even confessed to practising witchcraft, but after a few weeks of exhausting searching she had found a very special lady, someone who had also witnessed the creature as it snatched her husband's life away right before her eyes.

After weeks of emails and phone calls they had struck up a friendship. They had been able to discuss what happened to their husbands and Lilly Anne had found someone who understood the guilt and grief she felt just about every waking moment. Now, Bertha wanted them to meet and she had asked Lilly Anne to come to San Francisco. She had some information about the evil creature that she wanted to share.

At first, Lilly Anne had been a bit unsure about making the trip. A part of her wanted to know more about the creature that had stolen her husband and another part of her was scared that she might be told something that would traumatise her more.

Now though she had changed her mind. With the nightmares coming every night, Lilly Anne knew that she needed to know more about what had happened to her husband. She needed to know why the creature had picked him from all the other patients in the hospital. Why it had killed him and if it would be coming back for her, but most of all she had to know if her unborn baby was safe.

She placed her hands on her swollen pregnant abdomen. Junior was restless and it felt as if he was performing somersaults in her womb.

'I am keeping you awake again, honey,' she whispered to her unborn baby as she gently rubbed her stomach. 'Mommy won't be long then we can go back to bed and try to get some sleep.' She knew the sleepless nights would also be taking a toll on her baby.

The gentle soothing rubbing of her hands seemed to calm the baby and the movement started to subside.

In around five weeks' time she would give birth to James's son. The son he had always wanted but would never know. She had found out she was pregnant on the same day that James had been diagnosed with terminal cancer. She had chosen not to tell him about the baby, as she knew it would have broken his heart.

Sorrow engulfed her as she thought of her son becoming fatherless before he was even born. How she wished James could have lived long enough just to see him once, to have witnessed the birth and been able to hold James Junior in his arms for just a moment.

Lilly Anne sighed and gently patted her stomach. Maybe her son would never meet his father but it didn't mean he would never know him. Every day since James's death she had talked about him to her unborn child. She would tell the baby about James's short but full life and how wonderful and special he had made her feel. She would also tell the baby how much his father would have loved and treasured him and how he would be watching over him from heaven.

With the computer ready to use, Lilly Anne started typing an email. Once she had completed the document she hit the send button. She knew that Bertha would probably be up too, she also found it hard to sleep.

Switching off the computer she thought about Bertha. She hoped Bertha had something positive to tell. Hopefully she would be able to tell her that she had nothing to worry about, that her fears for her unborn baby were unfounded. She had to know her baby was safe. She had to know that the creature would not come back to claim him too.

'We had better try and get some rest,' she said out loud to her baby and she got up from the seat and headed back to bed. 'We have to be up early. We are going on a little trip.'

CHAPTER FIVE

March 2014
San Francisco

Bertha Cosgrove was busy preparing coffee for her four guests. She was glad that Lilly Anne had agreed to join them.

'Do you need a hand?' Juliet asked from the kitchen door.

She had been standing there practically since she'd arrived. She looked nervous and tired and Bertha felt sorry for her.

'No that's okay. You go and join the others.' Bertha smiled. Her ebony-wrinkled face was quite a contrast to her pure white Afro hair.

Bertha shuffled over to the refrigerator, her ample bosom swaying as she moved her bulky body around the room.

'Does everyone take milk?' she shouted through to the adjoining sitting room.

'Yes,' her guests answered in unison.

Bertha poured milk into each mug that already contained a spoonful of instant coffee before filling them with boiling water from the kettle. She added a jar of cookies and a freshly baked pie to the tray before making her way back to her visitors.

She placed the tray on the old, worn, coffee table and passed out the mugs to her two female and two male visitors.

'Would anyone like a cookie?' she asked passing the canister around. 'I just baked them this morning.'

Once her guests had been made to feel welcome, Bertha lowered her hefty body into a well-used armchair.

'I am so glad you could all make it here.' She beamed, her hazel eyes shining with happiness. 'It has been such a long time since I have had any visitors.'

'Thank you for having us,' Lilly Anne replied while secretly hoping she hadn't made the long trip to San Francisco just to keep an old woman company.

'So you have some information for us?' Graham Granger impatiently asked.

'I knew you wouldn't waste your time in getting to the point,' Bertha replied before taking a big bite from a chocolate-chip cookie. 'These are my favourite,' she said before gulping down some coffee. 'So what do you want to know about the beast?'

'Everything you know,' Graham replied in an impatient tone.

Lilly Anne turned her attention from Bertha to Graham. He reminded her of James, in some ways. He had the same charming, handsome face and the golden-coloured hair but he didn't seem to possess the same gentle nature.

'I want you to tell me everything you know. Maybe you could start with telling me what exactly killed my wife and where the heck it came from.'

'Sounds like a sensible place to start,' Patrick added as he sat on a sofa between Graham and Juliet.

Bertha looked around the room at the four eager faces, she had their full attention. 'What I have to tell you may upset you.' She focused her attention on the heavily pregnant Lilly Anne.

'Don't worry about me,' Lilly Anne reassured Bertha. 'I need to know.'

Bertha seemed to hesitate for a moment.

'Very well then,' Bertha said as she put her empty mug on the table. 'How many of you believe in the supernatural? How many of you think that witches, ghosts, demons and vampires exist?'

'Up until Simon's death I didn't believe in anything like that. I didn't even believe in God or the Devil but now I'm not so sure,' Patrick confessed.

'So what are you trying to say?' Graham dryly asked. 'That it was some kind of ghoul that killed my wife.'

'No it was something a lot worse than that.' Bertha leaned forward in her chair. 'What you all witnessed was the work of a soul-devouring demon.'

'I think you're wrong,' Juliet pitched in. 'I have carried out my own research and any references to soul-eating demons just don't match what I saw.'

'I agree with Juliet,' Lilly Anne added.

'Yes there are many soul-eating demons. The ones you have probably become familiar with or read about are the Kephn, floating demons known to the Karen tribes of Burma and the Phi Krasue demon of Thailand that consists of a head and some entrails. Of course there are many more who are similar in appearance to the two I have just mentioned.'

'I'm impressed,' Patrick joked as he tried to lighten the dark atmosphere. 'You really know your undead.'

Bertha smiled, the wrinkles on her face becoming even more prominent as she beamed.

'So if it's not any of the demons we know of then what is it?' Lilly Anne asked.

Bertha's smile vanished and her face was full of seriousness. This was no joking matter and she wanted to make sure that her visitors understood.

'The demon that we have all encountered is something special. These creatures have escaped from the very bowels of hell and wander the planet in search of souls.'

'You think it was a demon.' Graham shook his head in disbelief, he already looked as if he had heard enough.

'I don't know how many of you are practising Christians or believe in God.'

'Why? What has God got to do with Simon's death?' Patrick asked slightly confused. 'I thought God was the one that created man, not the one who wanted to take people away long before they should.'

Bertha raised her hand as if she were telling Patrick to be quiet.

'Is anyone familiar with the Nephilim?'

Silence from her visitors made it obvious that no one had a clue what she was speaking about.

'Not long after Adam and Eve had sinned,' she continued, 'Satan or the Devil, whatever you want to call him, was banished from heaven. Up until that day he was one of God's chosen ones, much like a son I suppose.'

'So what happened to him when he was removed from heaven?' Juliet asked her voice full of intrigue.

'He basically took up residence on earth until he was also banished from there.'

'I take it eviction saw the creation of the zip code 666,' Graham joked, not believing a word that was coming out of Bertha's mouth.

'If you are referring to the beginning of hell, then you are right,' Bertha replied tartly, knowing that Graham was mocking her.

'So who or what are the Nephilim?' Lilly Anne asked trying to stop any ugliness erupting.

'When Satan was banished so were some of his heavenly evil followers, fallen angels to you and I. These angels liked the look of the women that now populated the earth, the offspring of Adam and Eve. They had sexual relations with the females of the planet and the offspring of this unnatural union were known as the Nephilim.'

'So what were these children like?' Patrick asked, hoping the story was leading somewhere.

'The children grew like no earthly babies. At puberty they were more than eight feet tall and had the strength of an ox. Their souls were pure evil, full of hatred for human kind. They would maim or kill anything that stood in their way. They raped, pillaged and murdered hundreds of innocent individuals.'

'So basically they were homicidal maniacs with superhuman strength. Could they also fly?' Graham mocked. 'Didn't they star in a *Superman* movie?'

'Graham, please let Bertha continue,' Lilly Anne begged. 'So what happened to these unfortunate children?' she asked feeling sorry for the Nephilim, the unwanted and unnatural offspring of biblical creatures.

'One day they just disappeared.' Bertha's distaste in Graham's jokes evident in her voice as she looked at him in disgust.

'The Bible documents that they were wiped out by the great flood that saw only the survival of Noah and his family.

Historians, mythologists and pagans believe that Satan summoned them to the realms below.'

'So what are you trying to say? Do you think that these soul-eating creatures are the Nephilim? That they are creatures as ancient as the Bible itself?' Patrick asked with disbelief in his voice.

'No, I don't think that they are these creatures. They are the offspring of the Nephilim, beasts that have been born in hell itself. They are the children of demonic sexual relations, damned creatures that have been carved from evil itself. These beings know no mercy. They are monsters that have been born with a hunger for human souls.'

'I'm sorry but I don't think I can listen to any more of this bullshit,' Graham said as he got to his feet. 'You expect me to believe that one of Satan's minions was actually responsible for my wife's death?'

'You came here to find out the truth of what happened to your loved ones. I told you that you might not like what I have to say,' Bertha said as she leaned back into her chair and folded her arms around her heaving chest. 'If you don't want to listen any more, you know where the door is.'

'Graham, let her finish,' Lilly Anne said as she looked up at him. Her attractive, sweet face helped to calm Graham down.

'Okay, I will listen to what you have to say, but it doesn't mean I believe a word you have to say,' Graham said before taking his seat again.

'Please continue, Bertha,' Lilly Anne said, hoping that Bertha was willing to carry on after Graham's angry outburst.

'This soul-eating demon doesn't just hunt out any soul. No, the souls that he craves and devours are those of troubled and tortured individuals.'

'Do you mean it feeds on sad and unhappy people?' Patrick enquired.

'The people aren't just sad or unhappy. There is a unique quality to their grief,' Bertha continued. 'The victim will be suffering from heartbreak.'

Lilly Anne sat quietly in her chair. She felt numb inside. She clutched her pregnant stomach with both hands. 'Does it matter what has caused the heartbreak?'

Bertha nodded her head. 'Are you all right, Lilly Anne? Do you want us to take a short break for a moment?'

Lilly Anne could feel everyone looking at her. 'No I'm fine, please continue.'

'Are you sure?' Graham asked placing a concerned hand on her arm.

'Honest I'm fine.' She smiled back into his warm, friendly eyes. He really was very handsome and maybe she had been wrong about his nature, sure he seemed to be a bit hot-headed but he also seemed to be genuinely concerned for her well-being.

'So what has caused the heartbreak?' Juliet asked getting the conversation flowing again. Her anxiety evident by her tightly clenched hands and the continual biting of her bottom lip.

'Love, or should I say the lack of it.' Bertha leaned forward in her seat again, her eyes wide and her face full of expression. 'The victim will have announced their love for another human being. This expression of love will have been spoken out loud so that the recipient can respond.' She leaned back in her chair again, her wrinkled brown face full of sadness. 'If the recipient doesn't return the expression of love then...' Her voice trailed off, she knew she did not need to say any more.

'Then the person is filled with grief. They think that they are no longer loved and cannot bear the rejection and loss,' Lilly Anne finished for her as a tear ran down her cheek.

'Yes,' Bertha gravely confirmed. 'The grief that is emitted as the soul and heart are breaking can be heard by the demon. It sends the beast into a frenzy as it searches out the tortured victim.'

'I don't think you are right. I told my wife I loved her just before it killed her,' Graham added as he passed Lilly Anne a tissue from the box that sat on the coffee table.

'But did you mean it? Do you think your wife thought you meant it?' Bertha quizzed him.

Graham didn't say anything for a few moments. His complexion drained of colour as he thought of that fateful night.

'I didn't mean it,' he said looking defeated. 'I was actually about to leave her,' he continued. 'It happened a year ago just days before my thirty-fifth birthday. I had hired a private eye.' He turned his attention to Lilly Anne, his eyes searching for her support and understanding. 'She had been having an affair. It turned out to be with my best friend.'

Lilly Anne reached out and took hold of one of Graham's hands. She knew how he was feeling. He also blamed himself for the death of his partner.

'I came home to confront her. She was sitting in the bedroom. She had been crying. She knew I had found out about the affair and she swore that she had ended it.' He gave Lilly Anne's hand a gentle squeeze. 'She begged me to forgive her. She actually got down on her knees and pleaded.'

The group watched as Graham took a deep breath before continuing his story.

'I couldn't stand it any more. I just wanted to get out of the house, to get as far away from my cheating wife as possible.' He turned his attention to Lilly Anne again. His lips were dry and his eyes wet.

'When she told me she loved me, I didn't care if she really meant it. I could no longer stand the sight of her. I just returned the words to stop her from crying.' He finally released Lilly Anne's hand. 'She must have known that I didn't mean it.'

'She must have.' Bertha backed him up. 'It was the exact same with my husband. For years I had to put up with his many mistresses calling the house or turning up at the front door.' Bertha sighed. 'I was a very forgiving and understanding wife and it took me a long time to finally fall out of love with him.'

'But I hadn't stopped loving my husband,' Lilly Anne interrupted. 'I panicked when he unexpectedly woke up from the coma, I just couldn't bring myself to say the words.'

'Don't blame yourself, sweetie,' Bertha said trying to make Lilly Anne feel better.

'But I killed him. It was my fault, all my fault,' she said the tears now flowing freely.

'No it's not,' Graham said, his tone soft and warm. 'The demon is to blame for your husband's death.'

'Graham is right, Lilly Anne. The creature wants you to feel guilty. It wants you to take the blame for the death. It craves your grief. That is why a lot of the killings are staged as suicides.'

'Like Simon's death,' Patrick said grimly. 'I thought he killed himself because I didn't love him. For months I didn't think I could cope with my guilt and grief. I didn't get out of bed, didn't wash or eat and wouldn't speak to anyone. If my neighbour hadn't finally knocked down the door and helped me, I wouldn't be here today.'

'And that's exactly what the demon wants,' Bertha said. 'It wants all of us dead.'

'Why?' Lilly Anne asked as she wiped away the tears that were freely flowing. 'Hasn't it made us suffer enough?'

'It enjoys seeing us all suffer. It thrives on our personal pain. It's pure evil. It is nothing more than a satanic being that has the power to destroy life. In most cases the people who are left behind, the ones that witnessed the death are so caught up in their grief and guilt that they end their lives. Exactly what the beast wants.'

'What happens if its intended victim escapes? Will it try again?' Juliet asked, her voice full of anxiety.

Lilly Anne had nearly forgotten about Juliet. She had been sitting quietly for so long.

'It can only come back if circumstances dictate.'

'You mean if I don't confirm my love to my son.'

Bertha nodded. 'Your son was a very lucky little boy. Not many people survive when the creature closes in for a kill.'

'How old is your son?' Lilly Anne asked Juliet.

'He's nearly five.'

'Jesus,' Graham cursed under his breath, he felt sick at the thought that a child could have been killed in the same manner as his wife.

'It even hunts children.' Lilly Anne couldn't believe what she was hearing.

'As I said earlier, it's pure evil. It doesn't care about the age or the sex of its victim. Colour, creed and religion play no part in the type of soul the creature feeds on.'

'So what happens when it doesn't get its meal?' Graham enquired.

'I imagine it becomes pretty pissed,' Patrick added. 'I doubt it's happy when it doesn't get its own way.'

'No, it isn't pleased, in fact it becomes enraged. It will go and hunt out the next victim with even more venomous hatred and hunger.'

'So how many of these creatures have escaped?' Lilly Anne asked. 'Is it likely that the same one was responsible for all these deaths?'

'Most probably. From what I have found out, I think the same demon killed all our loved ones. I think there could be up to ten wandering the planet at this time. Yet I don't think that any of them feed in the same area. They seem to be solitary creatures, territorial and they don't hunt in a pack. It appears they all have their own designated feeding perimeter.'

'What makes you think that there are so many of these creatures?' Juliet asked with fear in her voice. She looked petrified.

'There have been sightings of these demons in many countries including France, Spain, the United Kingdom and Japan.'

'Has anyone actually got a good look at it?' Graham enquired. 'When it emerged from my wife's body it was nothing more than a grey shadow. I could make out its shape and form but I have no idea as to its facial features.'

'How did it appear to you, Lilly Anne?' Bertha questioned.

'Much the same as it did to Graham. At first I thought it was just a shadow being cast on the wall, it wasn't until it started moving that I realised that it was some kind of being.'

'It was more than a shadow that I saw,' Juliet pitched in. 'There seemed to be a form to the mist, like it was a being. It was really tall. It towered over Lennox and I.' She shuddered as she thought of the creature. 'I thought it was going... it was going to attack us.'

'Were you able to see what it looked like? Could you make out a face, a form?' Bertha enquired.

'No. It was just a tall, misty figure, as if it were not properly formed.' Juliet sighed and rubbed her temple. 'I'm sorry I can't be any more help, most of the time I had my eyes shut.'

'Don't you apologise.' Bertha smiled. 'The only reason I asked is because there has only ever been one person who has actually really seen the beast.'

'So what did he say it looked like?' Patrick asked.

'He didn't. He didn't live long enough to give anyone any kind of description. He did live long enough to give a brief statement but the details are very vague. A few minutes after the beast had tried and failed to take his wife, the creature appeared to him in its true form,' Bertha said grimly. 'Whatever he saw scared the life out of him. A few hours later he was dead. He died from a massive heart attack that had been induced by fear.'

'Poor man,' Lilly Anne whispered. She didn't think she could listen much longer. Bertha's tale was becoming more macabre by the minute.

Lilly Anne got to her feet. She needed some air and to stretch her legs. 'I'm just going to go outside and get some fresh air.' Bertha's old chairs were lumpy and uncomfortable, and were not doing much good for her pregnant form.

'Sure, honey. While you do that I will go and make us some fresh coffee, I'm sure we could all use a cup,' Bertha said as she heaved her large, flabby body from the seat.

Lilly Anne made her way out to Bertha's rickety old porch. The small, white wooden house was in dire need of a fresh coat of paint. Lilly Anne took a seat on one of the white, woven porch chairs. It was a beautiful spring evening. There was just a light, cool breeze that helped revive her wearied body and mind.

Lilly Anne rubbed her tense forehead. Her head was beginning to throb. She knew it was the beginning of a headache. There had been so much to take in. Bertha had been able to supply so much information about the creature, a lot more than she had expected.

'How are you bearing up?' Graham asked as he opened the porch screen and wandered out to join Lilly Anne.

'I'm okay. The baby has been a bit restless though. I had to get up before he kicked his way out,' she joked as she rubbed her stomach.

'So when are you due?' Graham enquired as he leaned against the crooked porch railing, his arms folded against his chest and his eyes focused on her face. He was dressed in dark blue jeans, a pale grey sweatshirt and a pair of black shoes. He had strong, handsome features and a lovely smile.

'Five weeks.'

'You must be really looking forward to the birth.' He warmly smiled.

'Yes I am.' She tried to smile back. 'I only wish his father could have lived long enough to see him.'

'I'm sorry,' Graham said as he moved towards her, his tall masculine frame towering above her. He placed an understanding hand on her shoulder. 'Just because he isn't here in the flesh, it doesn't mean he's not in spirit.'

Lilly Anne gazed back up into Graham's eyes. She could feel her pulse racing and her breath quickening. 'We had better get back inside,' she said as she abruptly got to her feet. She shouldn't be feeling attraction for this man she hardly knew. Her husband had only been dead six months and she was heavily pregnant with his child.

Graham held the door open for her as the pair made their way back into the dimly lit sitting room. He found Lilly Anne very attractive, even in her pregnant state. He wondered what she would say if he asked her out to dinner.

CHAPTER SIX

'So is there anything else you can tell us about the demon?' Patrick asked as he placed his mug on the table in front of him.

'What else would you like to know?'

'I want to know more about what happens when the creature enters the victim's body,' Patrick continued. 'How much would Simon have suffered?'

'I don't think he would have been in much pain,' Bertha answered. 'When the beast enters a human body, it takes control of the person. The victim becomes like a puppet and the beast will make it do whatever it wants as it begins consuming the soul. When your friend Simon jumped into your swimming pool, he would have known nothing about it. He would have been in a hypnotic trance, obeying the demon's every command.'

'What about my husband?' Lilly Anne wasn't so sure that Bertha was right. 'His death certificate states that he died of internal bleeding, he practically drowned in his own blood. I'm no doctor but I think he would have felt substantial pain and suffering before he finally passed away.'

'As I said he would have been in a hypnotic state, all his bodily functions and brain activity would have been controlled by the demon. He wouldn't even have known that the creature was inside him.'

‘So there is no hope of a strong-willed individual being able to fight off the demon, stop it controlling them and devouring their soul?’ Patrick added defeated.

‘Even if the victim was aware that the demon had entered their body there is no way they could stop it from killing them. It would be far too strong for any mere mortal to control. Remember this is a demon, an unearthly creature with superhuman strength. While the creature is in the spirit state, no one on earth has the power to stop it.’

‘So when is it not in a spirit state?’ Graham asked with intrigue in his voice.

‘Only when it appears in its true form.’

‘Like when that man died?’ Lilly Anne enquired.

Bertha nodded to confirm Lilly Anne’s words.

‘So how do we kill the demon when it manifests as a creature, as a complete being?’ Graham asked solemnly.

‘Are you serious?’ Patrick asked in surprise. ‘Would you really like to go up against that thing?’

Graham’s sombre face made it quite clear that he wouldn’t think twice about taking on the demon.

‘Why not? Didn’t Bertha say that this thing would keep watching us? How it has been wallowing in our hurt and pain. This demon isn’t going anywhere in the near future.’ The anger was blazing in his eyes as he turned his attention towards Juliet. ‘Especially seeing how it failed in one of its attempts. Do you really think your son is safe now?’

Juliet covered her face with her trembling hands. ‘Please don’t go on. I can’t stand the thought of that beast returning for my baby.’

‘I’m sorry for upsetting you, Juliet, but you know I’m right. No one in this room is safe and neither is anyone else in California. Innocent people will continue to die. The ones left behind will have their lives destroyed,' Graham said, his sobering words creating an atmosphere of dread.

'But it's not like killing a person. This thing is supernatural. It's not from our world. For all we know it's probably immune to bullets and other weapons,' Patrick added.

'Is he right ,Bertha?' Lilly Anne asked.

'I don't know if it can be destroyed, there are no records of anyone having gone up against one of these demons, but then again, I haven't really been looking for that kind of information.'

'Then maybe you should start looking,' Graham said.

'Do you really think that we should?' Juliet asked, her voice sounding small and frightened. 'If this thing is still watching us, do you not think it will find out that we are looking for ways to extinguish it?'

She looked around the room as if she expected the creature to appear at any moment.

'I'm with Juliet,' Lilly Anne added. She was starting to feel very anxious and tense. She never thought for one minute that her quest for more information on the being would lead her into danger, not only her but also her unborn child. 'I don't think the demon will be very happy with us. In fact how do we know that it wouldn't come after us if it found out what we were doing?'

'It doesn't work like that,' Bertha said trying to bring calm to the fear-charged atmosphere. 'Yes the demon could appear to you, maybe try and frighten you but it couldn't touch you unless circumstances dictate.'

'I hope you're right, Bertha, not for just my sake but also for the sake of the innocent lives that are involved,' Patrick interrupted her. His unhappy eyes fell on Lilly Anne's swollen abdomen.

'Everyone in this room is innocent!' Graham snapped out making the rest of the group jump. 'Don't you see, this thing expects us to be afraid. It enjoys seeing us suffer and probably gets a good kick out of our sleepless nights.'

He looked around at the scared faces and let his focus fall on Lilly Anne's sweet face. 'This thing has to be stopped. I couldn't live with myself if I found out that it had succeeded in taking a small child's soul.'

The group sat in silence for what seemed a very long time to Lilly Anne. She could tell by the expression on Patrick's face that he didn't want to go along with Graham's plan.

'At this time none of us have any information on how we would go about trying to kill this creature, am I right?' Lilly Anne said trying to break the unnerving silence. 'And I don't think anyone knows much about the creature in its natural form. So before we sit here and plan hunting and destroying it, wouldn't it be best for some of us to carry out some research? Then if we do come across some evidence or information to prove that this thing can be destroyed, then we can deliberate over the actual killing of it.'

'I agree,' Bertha pitched in. 'Tomorrow I will start looking into why the creature had manifested itself to that poor man. There had to be some special reason for it,' she continued, her face full of thought as if the wheels of her mind had started turning over some information that she had previously discarded.

'Patrick and I will start looking for evidence that this demon can be destroyed. Bertha, you can maybe give us details of some useful websites that will help get us started,' Graham added, eager to get things going.

‘We will also have to find out where this thing is hiding,’ Patrick gravely added. ‘It has to go somewhere between meals.’

‘Do you not think it would go back to hell? Is that not the perfect place to hide?’ Juliet asked.

‘I doubt that,’ Bertha said shaking her head. ‘It escaped from hell, I doubt it would return for fear that it might not escape again.’

‘I agree,’ Graham added. ‘But it must hide somewhere that is uninhabited, remote and secluded. Patrick and I will also do some geographical research.’

‘So what do you need us to do?’ Lilly Anne asked regarding herself and Juliet, the only ones that hadn’t been allocated a task yet.

‘Nothing at the moment,’ Graham said. ‘Juliet, you have your son to think of. If this thing finds out what we are doing the last thing you would need is the demon turning up at your house.’

‘Yes, I could do without that. Lennox has just started to sleep in his own room again. Goodness knows what would happen if he saw that evil creature again.’

‘As for you, Lilly Anne, I think you know why I don’t want the demon visiting you,’ Graham continued.

‘I know,’ she replied placing a hand on her baby bump. ‘But as soon as any of you have any information, please let me know.’

‘You and Juliet will be the first to know of any progress we make,’ he said while smiling reassuringly. There was no way he would have put her in harm’s way.

‘Better still, as soon as we have any information, I will arrange another meeting like this one,’ Bertha added.

‘Let’s make it at my home next time,’ Lilly Anne said as she got to her feet. ‘I don’t think I will be up to any more trips soon.’

The rest of Bertha’s visitors got to their feet. The first demon meeting was adjourned.

‘Bertha, you must stay with me when you visit,’ Lilly Anne added as Graham helped her into her coat. She knew the old woman didn’t have much money and would find it difficult to afford even a cheap motel room.

‘Thank you, Lilly Anne, I humbly accept your invitation.’ Bertha smiled as she hoisted her heavy frame from the creaking armchair.

The group made their way to the porch door saying their goodbyes as they went.

Lilly Anne made her way down the porch stairs into the cool spring evening. The sun had long disappeared and the dark, cloudy sky’s only source of light came from a heavily veiled, crescent moon.

‘So are you travelling home tonight?’ Graham asked her as he looked at his watch. It was now ten o’clock at night.

‘No I think I will book myself into a motel. I remember seeing one not far from here.’

‘Sounds like a good idea. Maybe I will join you,’ Graham said. ‘Separate rooms of course,’ he added as he watched Lilly Anne’s face blush.

‘What about you two, are you staying the night here?’ Lilly Anne asked Patrick and Juliet.

‘I have to get back for my son. My neighbour is babysitting,’ Juliet said as she gave Lilly Anne an unexpected hug before getting into her car. ‘I look forward to seeing you again soon. It’s nice to meet up with people who understand what I have been going through.’

Lilly Anne waved goodbye as Juliet drove off into the distance. She knew that there would be no sleep tonight. The fact that the demon had tried to take Juliet's son filled her with terror as she thought of her own unborn child.

'I have to head home tonight too. I have an early photo shoot in the morning.' Patrick extended his hand to Graham. 'Good luck with the digging, as soon as I have found anything I will let you know.'

Graham shook Patrick's hand. 'I'll do the same.'

Patrick got into his silver, Mercedes convertible. 'And if the beast pays you an unexpected visit, don't go giving it my new address,' he joked before he sped off at high speed.

Lilly Anne and Graham stood together in the ill-lit, quiet street. The wind was starting to pick up and a sudden chill made Lilly Anne shudder.

'We had better get you checked into that motel,' Graham said as he gestured towards her car. 'It's a bit cold out here.'

Lilly Anne allowed Graham to be the gentleman as he helped her into her car.

'You had better lead the way,' he said as he closed the door.

CHAPTER SEVEN

March 2014
Riverside, California

Tina Pollack and Mike Greenway were quarrelling again. It had been their third argument in the last two days and now Tina's temper was beginning to rise. She knew she would blow a gasket if Mike didn't shut up.

They had been arguing about the same subject and Tina wished Mike would give it a rest. He kept saying the same things over and over again. Maybe he thought that his repetition would finally make her give in to his demands.

She sat quietly in the car, her arms folded tightly across her chest, her eyes focused straight ahead into the dark, motionless trees and vegetation. They had parked in a quiet country spot just outside town. A place they used to come to make out.

'Are you even listening to me?' Mike barked at her, throwing his hands up in the air. 'I don't know why I even bother. Sometimes I don't think you even care about what this will do to our relationship.'

Tina continued to ignore him. She wasn't even going to start reasoning with him until he calmed down. It looked like it was going to be a long evening. Once Mike got on his high horse there was little chance of her talking him back down from his high and mighty, lofty position.

'Cleveland!' he angrily exclaimed as he ran a hand across his close-cropped brown hair. 'Do you know just how far away that is?'

Tina let out a sigh. Why couldn't he see that Cleveland College had the best facilities for her? She wanted to study art, something she had been passionate about for years. Her arts and crafts teacher thought she was a gifted artist with natural talent. It was actually Mr Smithy that had forwarded samples of her work to Cleveland. If it hadn't been for his faith in her, she wouldn't have been offered the scholarship.

'I will come and visit you as often as I can and there is nothing to stop you from making the trip to Cleveland when you want to see me,' she said as she folded her arms more tightly and continued to look ahead. There was no way she was giving in. Just because he had accepted a place right here in Riverside, didn't mean that she had to.

'We talked about this. We both agreed we would attend college here,' he continued to argue. 'You know I have to stay in Riverside. My father needs my help with the farm.'

'Yes I did agree that we would attend Riverside but that was before this chance came up. Can't you see this is an offer of a lifetime!'

She was really angry now and she turned her face to meet his, her emerald-green eyes blazing with anger. 'I am not doing this because I want to hurt you. I don't want to break up with you and I will miss you as much as you will miss me, but it is something I have to do,' she continued more calmly as she reached out and ran a finger down Mike's handsome, stubbly cheek.

Mike moved his face out of Tina's reach. He looked sad and dejected. 'I don't think I believe you,' he said in a small voice that was filled with hurt as he slumped in his seat. Mike knew Tina loved him but he was hurting, he couldn't bear the thought of her being so far away and not seeing her every day. He knew he was being an ass but he wanted her to feel his pain.

How could someone as big and burly be so soft on the inside, Tina thought to herself. If any of his jock friends had seen the six-foot-three, quarterback now, they would never have believed it was the same brutal, strong player that saved the team so many times on the football field.

'I have an idea,' Tina said trying to lighten the mood. 'Why don't you come down to Cleveland with me this weekend? I can show you round my dorm.' She edged closer to him again, her short, petite, slender frame a stark contrast to his large, manly body. 'Then maybe we can try out my bed, see if it will be able to handle your visits,' she continued as she ran a hand along and up one of his jean-clad legs, allowing it to rest on his groin.

Mike turned to look at her. His chestnut-brown eyes couldn't hide the sorrow that he was feeling inside and she loved him dearly, even when he was being such a jackass.

He leaned towards her and kissed her passionately. Her lips parted instinctively as his tongue began exploring her mouth. She gently squeezed his manhood and was pleased to see that he was aroused. Allowing his hand to open her blouse she began reclining the seat as he lowered his head to her bosom and sought out one of her pert nipples. Tina groaned loudly, he could turn her on so easily.

'I can't do this,' Mike said as he moved away from Tina. 'This isn't right.'

'What do you mean?' Tina asked surprised and slightly embarrassed as she tried to fasten the buttons on her gaping blouse.

'You and I won't last when you move away. Long-distance relationships never work. In a couple of months' time you will call me to tell me that it's over.'

'Don't be so stupid!' Tina blurted out. Her face as red as her hair as she felt the anger build again. 'We have been together for six years now. Do you really think so little of me?' She felt like slapping him. Couldn't he see just how much he was hurting her? 'For once will you stop thinking of yourself. Have you even considered how I am feeling?' She started getting into her jacket. 'This was the hardest decision I have ever had to make.'

'Yeah I bet it was!' Mike shouted back at her, his voice full of sarcasm.

'You are nothing more than a selfish, pig-headed creep,' she continued as she opened the car door. Tears had formed in her eyes and some were already spilling down her face. 'I just wish you would believe me when I say I love you and that I never want this relationship to ever end.'

She jumped out of Mike's station wagon and started walking in the direction of town.

Mike sat there in the quiet of the car for a few moments, his arrogant, alpha male thoughts still fuelling his stubborn pride. There was no way he was going after her, if she really loved him she wouldn't be moving to Cleveland.

Starting the engine he turned on the lights, the strong beam focusing on Tina as she haughtily walked ahead of the car, her feminine buttocks wiggling as she strutted away into the distance.

He loved her so much. He knew there was no way he could live without her. Putting the car into gear he drove the car until it was alongside Tina. Pressing a button he watched as the window lowered and Tina's wet face appeared more clearly before him.

'I'm sorry, Tina, you know I love you. I just can't stop feeling this way when I realise I won't see you every day.'

Tina stopped dead. 'Did you hear that? It sounded like a scream,' she asked with fear in her voice.

Mike stopped the vehicle and stepped outside. He wrapped his arms around his trembling girlfriend. 'It probably was a wild dog. Come on, let's get back in the car and finish what we started earlier,' he whispered huskily in her ear, pressing his hard, erect groin against her.

The pair jumped as a high-pitched screech sounded just feet in front of them.

'Don't move,' Mike warned as he pulled Tina tightly against him. 'That sounds more like a bear than a dog to me,' he whispered.

'Mike, I'm scared,' Tina whispered trying desperately to hold back the screams of terror she was keeping in. 'Shouldn't we try and get back into the car?'

Mike's legs were quivering and the hairs on the back of his neck were standing on end. He had never been this afraid before. 'When I say go, we will both turn and get into the car as fast as possible.'

'Okay,' Tina said barely able to reply. The sheer panic she was feeling had swept through her entire body and was now constricting her vocal cords.

'GO!' Mike yelled as he physically turned Tina and himself round to face the car. Tina didn't think her feet got a chance to touch the ground before Mike had practically thrust her into the front seats of the vehicle.

'Shut the door!' she squealed out as she clambered across the driver's seat allowing Mike to gain access to the vehicle.

Once inside Mike closed the door and locked it. At the same time Tina checked that her door was securely shut. Whatever was out there wasn't going to get to them too easily.

Another blood-curdling bellow made Tina scream out in dread. She was in fear for her life. That didn't even sound like a bear. Whatever was out there was moving closer to the parked car. 'Get the engine started! We have to get out of here!'

'I'm trying!' Mike replied as he slammed his hand against the steering wheel and turned the key in the ignition again. He sighed with relief as the engine finally roared into life.

'What the fuck!' Mike exclaimed as he looked ahead at the black swirling form making its way towards the car. At first he thought it was nothing more than a mini twister, or maybe even a big swarm of bees but as the dark, twirling mass continued its advance he knew that Mother Nature had nothing to do with the strange phenomenon.

The pair sat in stunned silence as they watched the shrieking and howling mass as it quickly encircled the entire vehicle.

'Give me her back,' something inside the cloud hissed as it continued its pulsating whirling around its terrified prey. 'She belongs to me now. You don't really love her. Tell her how much you hate her for leaving you and that you wish she were dead,' the voice continued, focusing its evil taunts at Mike.

'Go away!' Mike yelled. 'I love her more than anything in this world. You will never take her away from me. Now piss off whatever you are.'

'One day I will get her. One day you will stop loving her and then she will be mine,' the voice shrieked as the spinning furiously accelerated causing the entire vehicle to start rocking.

Tina started to hysterically scream as the passenger window exploded by the side of her face. Defensively she put her hands up to try and stop the small, sharp shards of glass from penetrating her face and neck.

'Tina!' Mike shouted out as he pulled her over to his side of the car and placed a strong, muscular, protective arm around her shoulders. He could see the glass had wounded her as it had exploded into hundreds of pieces. Both her hands were covered with tiny, red stained cuts.

'Don't go too far, Tina. You never know what may happen if you move away. Your beloved Mike won't be able to save you in Cleveland,' the fiendish voice taunted from deep inside the evil mass. 'Just remember I will be watching you.'

'Go to hell!' Mike shouted just as the black cloud dispersed and calming silence once again filled the air.

Raising a weary hand to his head, Mike wiped away the beads of sweat that had formed.

'Whatever it was, Tina, it's gone now,' he said as his eyes darted around the familiar countryside for any signs that the ghoulish mist was still in the vicinity.

Tina sat up. The right side of her face was smeared with blood. Her hands hadn't been quick enough and some of the window's glass had penetrated her cheek and chin.

‘We have to get you to the hospital,’ Mike said as he helped Tina back into her seat.

She was holding her bloody hands in front of her eyes, staring at the numerous gashes.

‘What was that?’ she asked trying to choke back the tears.

‘I don’t know and I don’t think I want to know,’ Mike said as he fastened her seat belt for her. ‘We really have to get you to the hospital and get those hands looked at,’ he continued as he lowered her hands and gently placed them in her lap. Taking his precious high school jacket off, he wrapped it around her trembling body. ‘I think you are also suffering from shock.’

‘And you’re not!’ she shouted. ‘I don’t know what kind of creature that thing was, all I know was that it was pure evil,’ she continued as she began to weep.

Mike didn’t know what to do to help calm Tina down. He just didn’t know what to think or say. He had never been so scared in his entire life. At one point he thought he might wet his pants. The creature that had been outside the vehicle had wanted Tina dead.

‘You know it was going to kill me?’ Tina said, as if she were reading his mind.

‘Yes,’ Mike answered before starting the car engine again as it had stalled during the attack. ‘Tina, we really have to get you to hospital,’ he said as he started slowly moving the vehicle back out of the woodland and on to the main road.

‘You saved me,’ she continued. ‘If you didn’t love me, I would be dead now.’

‘Don’t say things like that, Tina,’ Mike said as he placed a loving hand on one of her trembling, cold legs. He didn’t like to admit it but he knew she was right.

‘It said that you won’t be able to save me in Cleveland. How the hell did it know I was moving away?’ she asked in a wavering voice.

‘I don’t know, Tina,’ Mike admitted as he sped the car towards the hospital. At least the cuts to Tina’s face and hands looked superficial, hopefully she wouldn’t need too many stitches.

‘I’m not going now, I can’t go,’ she said in a small voice.

‘Not going where? If you are meaning the hospital you can think again. You really must have those cuts looked at,’ Mike said as he took a quick sideways glance at his injured girlfriend.

He was now moving at quite a speed and the gaping passenger window was allowing the cold evening breeze free access to the vehicle. Tina’s long, auburn hair was being tossed in every direction. Strands of her hair had come in contact with the sticky, crimson stream that was running down her face and were now encrusted with drying blood. To look at her now you would think she had been the victim of a terrible road accident.

‘I’m not going to Cleveland,’ she continued, as her trembling appeared to be worsening.

‘Don’t be silly. Of course you can still go. Those cuts on your hands don’t look too bad, I think the blood is making them look worse,’ he said trying to reassure her. ‘They will heal in no time and you will probably be able to start painting again in a couple of days.’

‘My hands aren’t the reason. Stop being so stupid!’ she yelled at him as she tried to choke back the tears. ‘It said it’s coming back for me. You won’t be in Cleveland to save me.’

Mike knew she was right. The thing had warned them that it would be back. It had made it quite clear that it wanted

Tina and if he was totally honest with himself, it did not really matter if Tina stayed with him in Riverside. He doubted he would be able to stop whatever had attacked them from hurting Tina again.

CHAPTER EIGHT

March 2014
O'Neil's Restaurant and Tavern
San Francisco

Graham Granger paid the young, smiling waitress. The small and dimly lit motel bar was very quiet. Mostly business reps dressed in cheap suits occupied a handful of the tables.

He made his way back to the table that Lilly Anne had selected in one of the secluded corners of the room. 'Here you go. An orange juice on the rocks,' he joked as he passed her the glass.

'Thank you.' She smiled as he took a seat beside her.

'No, thank you. If you hadn't agreed to a nightcap I would have been sitting here all alone.'

'Actually I'm glad you suggested this,' she said before taking a sip of the icy-cold, fruit juice. 'There is no way I would be able to sleep yet.'

'I know what you mean. It has been quite a day.'

Graham took a hearty swig of his cold beer. 'So, Lilly Anne, tell me some more about yourself. That is if you don't mind.' He hoped he wasn't coming on too strong or sounding overfamiliar, but he really was interested in getting to know more about her.

'No I don't mind,' she said with a cute smile. 'I am thirty-three years of age and up until the death of my late husband I worked as a realtor in Moreno Valley.' She looked down and patted her stomach. 'And once I have given birth to my son, I hope to return to my job on a part-time basis.'

Graham couldn't believe the resolve of this woman. It was obvious that she was a very determined and strong-willed individual. She had been through so much in the last few months. She had witnessed the death of her husband at the hands of a demon and had had to come to terms with the fact that she would be a single mother. Yet she continued to be strong and still had positive plans for the future.

'So tell me something about yourself,' Lilly Anne coaxed.

'Well, I am a thirty-five-year-old widower. As I said earlier today I lost my wife a few years ago. I am the owner of a small accounting firm. I have three offices in California but I am mainly based in the Riverside office.'

'Is that where you live?'

Graham nodded as he took a drink. 'I have lived in Riverside for about ten years now. It was where I met my late wife.'

Lilly Anne watched as she caught a quick glimpse of sadness in Graham's eyes. She could tell he still felt responsible for her death.

'So what do you think of Bertha?' she asked trying to change the subject.

'Now there's a God-fearing woman if I ever had met one,' Graham joked. He was glad Lilly Anne had not asked about his wife or about her affair.

'She really has conviction in her faith, but then again look at what she has been through. Her husband continually cheated on her. She has no money and a ramshackle home and then as if life hasn't been bad enough, she had to endure witnessing the death of her husband as an evil, unearthly creature devoured his soul right before her eyes. I think her belief in God and Jesus Christ gives her hope for the future and helps keep her sane.'

'Daily life must be a struggle for her,' Graham added. 'Yet even though she has been through so much personal pain she still invited us all to her home. She still wanted to help us understand what happened to our partners and loved ones and try and help us get over our guilt and grief.'

'I know. She really is a remarkable old woman.' Lilly Anne smiled. She felt so relaxed, so at ease and this was the first time she had really enjoyed another human being's company since the death of her husband.

'And there is something else about her that we shouldn't forget, probably her most endearing quality. One that all four of us found the most beneficial tonight.'

Lilly Anne raised an inquisitive eyebrow. 'Oh yeah, and what is that?'

'She bakes fantastic cookies.' Graham laughed.

The pair started to giggle loudly and neither of them could help or stop the hilarity. It was the first time in a very long time that Lilly Anne had found something to laugh about and even though it wasn't that funny she couldn't stop herself from chuckling out loud.

Lilly Anne tried to compose herself when she realised that they were drawing unwanted attention. A few drunken heads had raised and were quizzically gazing over to where they were seated.

Graham had also noted that they were being watched. 'So what do you think of Patrick and Juliet? Have you spoken to either of them before this evening?'

'I have communicated through email with Juliet a couple of times before today. As for Patrick I didn't know anything about him until tonight,' Lilly Anne replied as she finally regained her composure.

'Juliet is so frightened. I really feel for her. I bet she never stops telling that son of hers how much she loves him.'

'I think she is getting a bit better now. She told me that she was on the verge of becoming an alcoholic when it happened. As soon as the creature tried to steal her son she stopped drinking.'

'I think seeing that thing would be enough to sober up anyone,' Graham said as he finished his beer. 'Would you like another drink or am I imposing too much?'

'No I'm fine, you go ahead and have another one. I am no way ready for bed yet.'

'Good,' Graham said as he caught the attention of the waitress and ordered another beer. 'My mind is so alive. I still haven't taken in everything. When Bertha started spouting about a soul-eating demon, I just couldn't believe what she was saying. I was on the verge of walking out more than once. I have never believed in heaven, hell or the afterlife. The thought that such unearthly creatures could be inhabiting the earth just didn't sound like a logical explanation to me.'

'I know. I found it hard to believe what she was saying. I just didn't want to think that something so evil had taken James's life.'

'I don't think we were the only ones to find it hard to believe Bertha. I think Patrick wasn't so sure as well, but then again, I think Patrick is finding it very hard to cope with life in general,' Graham said as the waitress placed a fresh bottle of beer on the table.

'Cheers and keep the change,' he said to the smiling waitress as he passed her five dollars.

Lilly Anne waited for the young woman to leave before answering him. 'So you noticed it as well.'

Graham nodded. 'He was a quivering wreck the whole evening. I don't think that Bertha succeeded in persuading him that he wasn't to blame for his lover's death.'

'Maybe we should keep an eye on him,' Lilly Anne said, looking worried as she thought of Patrick. She was genuinely concerned for his welfare. He had joked and laughed at some of the things Bertha had told them as he tried to hide his fear and anxiety. 'Can you maybe give him a call tomorrow and see how he's doing.'

'No problem. I have to give him a call anyway to pass on the research details. Bertha is emailing me all the relevant websites tomorrow.'

'So will you begin the research tomorrow?'

Graham nodded. 'Tomorrow evening.'

'Remember you promised to keep Juliet and I informed of any important information you find.'

'Don't worry you will be the first to know,' Graham said. He knew she was itching to be involved.

'Are you sure there is nothing I can do to help? I feel like I'm being left out.'

'Lilly Anne, the only reason we don't want you doing any of the research is because we don't think it would be safe for you or the baby. We don't want the beast visiting you again, especially when you're alone.'

'Then I won't look into anything on my own. We don't live that far away from one another, is there no way I can maybe help you?'

Graham liked the sound of that. It would be the ideal chance for him to get to know Lilly Anne better. 'Okay then. Tomorrow evening we will work together, but if anything happens that frightens you...'

'Then I won't get involved further,' Lilly Anne finished for him. 'I'll give you my address and phone number tomorrow morning when we are checking out. Give me a call when you finish work and I will prepare us dinner before we start.'

Graham smiled. He was already looking forward to tomorrow night. 'Sounds good to me.'

CHAPTER NINE

March 2014
Santa Clara, California

'Patrick, you promised me,' Carlton whined into the phone. 'I thought we were going to spend the day together. You didn't come and see me last night and now you cancel on me again.'

'I'm sorry, Carlton but I forgot I had arranged to visit someone this morning. It is really important that I still go.'

'Who is more important than me?' Carlton was not amused at being blown off. 'I hope it isn't another man.'

'No, you are the only one I am seeing. Stop being so paranoid. If you must know I am going to see my mother.'

'Sorry, Patrick, I didn't mean to sound so untrusting. It's just that you have been acting so strange the last few days.'

'I know I have been a pain in the ass. I hope my mood swings haven't been too unbearable.'

'Don't worry about it. You have been through a lot in the last six months. You go and have a good time and I will see you tomorrow.'

'Thanks, Carlton,' Patrick replied before ending the call. If only Carlton had known what his mother was like, he would have stopped Patrick from making the visit.

It had been more than two years since he had seen his mother. It had been on the day of his father's funeral and she had made it quite clear that she didn't want anything more to do with her gay son.

'Your mother will be downstairs in a moment,' his mother's young, pretty-faced assistant said as she led him to the familiar family drawing room.

Patrick walked through the arched doorway and back in time. The place hadn't changed a bit. The walls were still adorned in the same pale pink, hand-painted wallpaper that had been imported from Japan and the family antiques and heirlooms stood as they always had on the many ornate, teak dressers and tables.

'Please take a seat and I will go and arrange tea for you and your mother,' the assistant nervously said before exiting the room. She knew that his mother would not welcome this unexpected visit.

Patrick took a seat on one of the cream and gold embroidered chairs. He hadn't been this nervous for such a long time and he had even dressed for the occasion. He had bought new black trousers, a pale blue shirt and navy blue tie, all designer of course. He felt rather overdressed but hoped that his mother would be pleased that he had made an effort.

'So what can I do for you?' his mother drawled as she entered the room.

Lydia Edwards was wearing a cream and black Coco Chanel suit and matching two-tone, stiletto-heeled shoes. Her jet black, dyed hair and make-up were as immaculate as ever and she still wore the same awful, light pink lipstick that did nothing for her pale complexion.

Patrick started to rise from his seat.

'Please don't get up on my account.' The arrogance in her upper-class voice letting him know that he wasn't welcome.

'You look well, Mother,' Patrick said and meant it. His mother still was a stunningly good-looking woman at the age of sixty-three years.

'Thank you, I suppose,' she said as she disinterestedly looked down at her perfectly manicured nails.

'Here's the tea,' the assistant announced as she carried in a tea tray. 'Do you need anything else?' she asked as she placed the tray on the coffee table that separated Patrick and his mother.

'No, you can leave us now and close the doors on your way out,' his mother ordered.

Patrick watched in silence as his mother poured two cups of tea from the china teapot. No doubt it would be Earl Grey, his mother's favourite.

'So tell me, Patrick, why have you come here? I thought I made it quite clear that you were no longer welcome in my home.'

'I was hoping that you might have changed your mind,' he replied as he watched her add milk and sugar to the china cups.

'What made you think that?' she asked as she passed him the cup on a saucer. 'I know you haven't changed your lifestyle,' she dryly added with distaste in her voice.

'I cannot help being what I am,' Patrick blurted out.

'Can't or won't? You are unnatural. What you do is disgusting and vulgar,' she said with even more venom. 'I am so ashamed of what you have become. Do you know what the neighbours say about you, or don't you even care?'

Patrick shook his head in disbelief. She was such a snob. Material possessions, wealth and standing in the community were all she cared about.

'I don't care about what the neighbours or your wealthy friends think of me,' Patrick said as he forcefully placed the cup and saucer back on the table causing them to loudly rattle. 'Dad didn't care about my sexuality and I thought that you had also accepted the man I have become.'

'I never agreed with your father. I couldn't believe it when he still accepted you as a member of this family. To think such an educated and powerful man would actually allow his son to carry on with such a despicable lifestyle is beyond belief,' she said as she continued her verbal attack. 'Maybe he could bear living with a disgusting, vile child that had blackened our name, but there was no way I could any longer. Goodness knows what diseases you could have passed on to me if I had allowed you to stay here any longer.'

'What did you just say?' Patrick practically shouted as he got to his feet. 'Do you think I am some kind of leper because I am gay?'

'You know fine what I mean,' Lydia coolly said. 'The day after your father was laid to rest, I arranged a doctor's appointment. I had to make sure that you hadn't passed on one of your homosexual diseases.'

Patrick laughed out loud in disbelief. 'You mean like Aids?' He couldn't believe it. His mother didn't know the first thing about his choice of life. 'You know what, Mother, I believe you are the biggest homophobe I have ever met.'

'And what is wrong with that?' she replied haughtily as she looked him up and down. 'I don't want to know anything about you or your kind.'

'Well, it's obvious you don't know much about me.' Patrick sank back down in the chair again. He felt so deflated. 'You seem to think I have been sleeping around and that I have been having sex with every Tom, Dick and Harry. Just because I am gay doesn't mean I am promiscuous.'

'So you say,' she bit at him, her eyebrows raised and her thin, pink lips tight.

'Yes I do say, Mother, and I wish you would believe me,' Patrick wearily said. 'I have only dated two men in the last year or so. That is probably a lot less than the amount of men that your sister has got through in the last few weeks.'

'Leave my sister out of this,' Lydia said trying not to raise her voice or look embarrassed. 'Don't you go speaking about Tanya. At least she hasn't been the cause of anyone's death.'

Patrick sat numbly in his chair. His mother's angry words had chilled him to the bone. It was obvious she had heard of Simon.

'I take it by your stunned silence that you know whom I am speaking of,' Lydia said triumphantly as she sat across from him.

Patrick wanted to wipe the smug, satisfied look off her face. 'Of course I know you are speaking about Simon. It's not as if I can ever forget that he is dead. After all, he did die at my home,' he sarcastically answered. 'So tell me, how did you find out about what happened?'

'I read about it in the newspaper. The same way as all my neighbours and friends found out. Do you know I didn't leave the house for days? I was so ashamed and embarrassed. I'm only glad your father isn't still around to see what kind of man you have become.'

'And what kind of man is that, Mother?' Patrick snapped back at her. If he didn't care for her so much he would have left by now, but he had come here to try and patch up their non-existent relationship. He wasn't going to leave until he had talked her into forgiving him.

'You are nothing more than a pervert. You seduced that poor young man. I wouldn't be surprised if you talked him into having sex with you. Once the poor boy realised what he had done he took his own life. He was so ashamed with himself for having unnatural sex with another man.'

'And you got all that from the newspaper article?' Patrick sarcastically asked her. 'I think you should tell me the name of the paper you read as I think I might just sue the editor's ass!' he loudly said as he leaned across the table to stare angrily into the eyes of the woman that had at one time been his loving mother.

'The article didn't exactly say all those things but it doesn't take a genius to read between the lines and come up with what really happened that night.'

'Do you realise what you are saying? You are basically accusing me of rape.' He couldn't believe that his own mother thought so little of him. 'At least Dad wouldn't have agreed with you, he would have known that I hadn't caused Simon's death.'

'Do you really think so? Maybe your father stood by you before but do you think he would have wanted anything to do with you after what has happened? You would have ruined his career. He would have been a laughing stock at the office.'

'You know that's not true.' Not everyone had the same warped mind as his mother. 'No one would have said a thing to Dad. You know he was one of the most respected members of the board.' Patrick knew he was fighting a losing battle. 'Do you really want to know why Simon took his own life, or are you not willing to hear my side of the story?'

'I already believe I know the truth but if it will speed up your departure then I am all ears,' she sarcastically drawled.

'As you have already guessed Simon and I were romantically involved. We had been dating for a few months.'

Patrick got to his feet again. He watched as his mother leaned back in her chair and crossed her slender legs. Her full attention was set upon him, her unbelieving and scrutinising stare making him feel as if he were being cross-examined in the Supreme Court.

'He was a very handsome, charming young man but I just didn't see our relationship progressing into something long-term.' He turned his back to his mother and nervously starting turning one of the crystal goblets that stood upon a dresser. He didn't want her to see how much guilt he was carrying or how upset he was for the death of Simon. 'So that evening I invited him to my house to tell him it was over. As you can imagine he didn't take it too well, in fact he fell apart right in front of me. He cried and begged me not to split up with him.'

Patrick turned back to face his mother. By the look on her face it was obvious she didn't believe a single word that was coming out of his mouth. 'I went downstairs to get him a drink, a shot of something to try and help him calm down.'

'You gave a drink to a minor?' Lydia disgustedly asked.

'Please let me finish, Mother,' Patrick asked although he didn't know why as it was obvious that she had already passed sentence. 'I never got the chance to give him the drink, when I returned to the room he was already gone. He had jumped out of the first-floor window and into the swimming pool below.'

'So did you try and resuscitate him?'

'At the time I panicked and at first didn't know what to do. I got him out of the water and called for medical assistance.' Patrick remembered how foolish he had felt for not knowing basic first-aid treatment. 'It wouldn't have done any good if I had tried to resuscitate him, drowning hadn't been the cause of his death.'

'Then what was?' his mother probed.

'He had broken his neck in the fall. He was already dead when he hit the water,' Patrick said flatly.

'So basically you are telling me he killed himself because of your rejection?' she said her voice full of mockery.

Patrick sighed. 'It wasn't just because I ended the relationship. Simon told me that he had fallen in love with me and that he wouldn't be able to go on with life if I stopped seeing him.'

'Oh it's a tale of unrequited true love. A modern *Romeo and Juliet*? Don't make me laugh. Do you know how incredible your story sounds?' Lydia said with a smug grin on her face.

'What's wrong, Mother? Do you find it hard to believe that gay love exists?'

'There is no such thing. True love can only exist between a woman and a man or between a parent and a child.'

'Like the love that exists between you and I?' Patrick scoffed. 'Yes – motherly love just flows from you.'

'Don't talk to me like that, Patrick! You have no right,' Lydia said rising to her feet in one swift motion. 'The day your father was laid to rest was the same day I lost my only son. You are no longer part of this family and I want you to leave right now.'

'So as I am no longer your son I can take it that you no longer love me either?' Patrick asked, his voice full of sorrow, as he already knew the answer.

‘Love you? You must be joking. I hate the man you have grown into. I hate the degrading and disgusting way of life you have chosen. I hate you and wish you were never born!’ Lydia shouted, her face crumpled with malice and her hands balled into fists as if she was ready to punch him.

Patrick stood staring at his hate-ridden mother for a few moments. He hoped that the demon had been listening. He hoped the demon had felt his pain.

When his father had died, he had been inconsolable for months. His father had been there for him, had supported him and accepted his sexuality. Patrick missed him so much that sometimes he still cried at the thought of never seeing him again.

Patrick turned to look at his mother again as he wondered if she would cry at his funeral. He wondered if she would feel the same loss, the same heartbreak.

‘So that’s it, Mum, you hate me so much you wish I were dead,’ Patrick said catching a dark shadow move its way across one of the walls towards him. He felt frightened, scared witless at the thought of the demon entering his body but he was ready to be taken, ready to die. He could no longer live with the guilt. Every day he thought about Simon and about his awful death. If only he had told Simon he had loved him, all he had to do was lie and Simon would still be here today.

‘The thing is, Mother, I don’t hate you. You can reject, denounce and disinherit me but it won’t change the way I feel about you. You are all I have left and I love you.’

Patrick turned his head towards the shadow. In a few moments the beast would be inside, controlling his every action and thought. He just had time to wonder about how he was going to die as he turned his back on his mother again.

'Don't you turn your back on me! I told you I wanted you out of my house now!' she shouted at the top of her voice. 'If you don't go in the next few seconds I will call the police,' she threatened.

Patrick felt no pain as the unearthly creature absorbed itself into his manly frame. His hand reached out and picked up one of the long-stemmed, crystal goblets that stood before him. The demon had taken total control of his body and mind.

Lydia watched in puzzlement as Patrick raised the glass above his head. In a fast and aggressive motion he brought the glass down hard against the dresser smashing it to pieces.

'What are you doing? Do you have any idea how much those glasses cost?'

The evil spirit deep within Patrick started its consumption of his tortured soul as it made him turn to face Lydia. His hand still had a firm grasp on the sharp protruding stem of the glass.

'Did you hear me?' she asked searching his expressionless face for an answer.

'I heard you, Mother dear,' the beast said using Patrick as a vessel to carry out its planned ghastly events that would haunt Lydia for the rest of her life. 'But I wish you would just shut the fuck up for once. I have something to say to you before I go.'

Lydia stood fixed to the spot. Fear and shock gripped her. Patrick had never before spoken or acted in such an aggressive manner. 'So what do you have to say?' Lydia asked her gaze transfixed on the remaining piece of glass that he was still gripping tightly.

'You are nothing but a snobby, self-centred cow,' Patrick said as he started to sway on his feet. It wouldn't be long before the beast would have devoured his entire soul. His death was only moments away. 'I came here today to ask for your forgiveness and support. I have found it so hard to cope with life since Simon's death.'

Lydia watched as Patrick's swaying worsened, she was sure he was about to faint or fall over.

'I wonder if you will be able to live with yourself after my death,' Patrick said as he raised the sharp end of the remaining glass towards his throat. 'Goodbye, Mother.'

Lydia screamed as she watched in horror as her son brutally rammed the glass shard into his neck severing the main artery as it punctured the skin and flesh. An uncontrollable spurt of blood erupted from the wound and splattered over the pale pink walls behind him.

Patrick slumped to the floor as the blood continued to escape from his body. Within moments the front of his shirt was soaked with blood and a burgundy pool had started to appear on the wooden floor beside his head. Crimson bubbles formed around his lips as he rasped his last few laboured breaths.

Lydia rushed across the room and knelt beside her injured son. Hesitantly she firmly grasped the wounded area trying to stop more blood from escaping. The entire front of her cream and black designer suit now stained pink. She called out as loud as she could to her assistant. 'Call an ambulance,' she shouted over and over again.

Her entire attention was focused on Patrick. 'Please don't die, son, please hold on until help gets here. I am so sorry for the things I said,' she wailed unaware that her son was already gone and that the creature that had killed him had already left his soulless body.

The demon's shadowy shape watched her from the drawing room window before making its escape. It wanted to taunt and goad her further, see how much it would need to push her before she took her own life, but that could wait for another time. The beast was tired. It would go and rest now that it was content and full.

CHAPTER TEN

March 2014
Moreno Valley, California

'Dinner looks wonderful,' Graham said as he walked into Lilly Anne's kitchen. The terracotta walls and spot lighting made the room feel warm and welcoming. 'And it smells delicious,' he continued his compliment as he took a seat on one of the two facing lattice benches that stood either side of a rectangular pine table.

Everything about the room said family. From the highly polished wooden floor to the spick and span work units, Graham could tell that Lilly Anne highly rated a good home life and was going to make a wonderful mother.

'Thank you.' Lilly Anne beamed. 'I hope you like your greens. I eat a lot of vegetables. They are good for the baby.'

'I love them now but I must confess that I hated them as a child,' Graham said as Lilly Anne passed him a steaming bowl of mashed potatoes. She had made enough to feed an army.

'So did you get the information from Bertha?'

'Yes she emailed the details to my office this morning. You should see all the information she has sent. She must devote most of her waking life to finding out more about the creature.'

'Have you had a chance to look at any of it yet?' Lilly Anne enquired between mouthfuls of food.

'I had a quick look through some of the files during lunch. She has found out a lot about the origin of the demons and details on where they have been sighted.'

'So do you think from the sightings you may be able to get a better fix on where this thing is hiding?'

Graham shrugged his shoulders and took another helping of the potatoes before smothering them in Lilly Anne's delicious gravy.

'I have a few ideas as to where this thing may be living but the only way we can find out if we are looking in the right place is to go and check the sites ourselves.'

'Are you sure that would be a good idea?' Lilly Anne could feel the fear rise in her at the thought of searching out the beast. 'I don't think this thing will be very happy if it finds you on its doorstep.'

'I know it doesn't sound the most sane thing to do but I don't think we have much choice. If we want to kill this thing then we have to find it and if we find a way to kill it then I don't think it will be so willing to pay us visits.'

Lilly Anne hadn't thought of that. She knew the beast was still watching them, waiting for the right time to taunt them and remind them of the pain and suffering it had caused. It had the power to do so. Yet would that power still exist when they had found a way to destroy it?

'Please promise me you will be careful,' Lilly Anne said. Her eyes intently focused on Graham's.

Graham reached across the table and squeezed Lilly Anne's hands tightly. 'I promise,' he said and meant it. He was so pleased that Lilly Anne cared for his well-being.

'Anyway I won't be going alone,' he continued as he released Lilly Anne's hands. 'I will be taking Patrick with me.'

'Does Patrick know that?'

'Not yet. I tried to speak to him earlier today. I called his studio and home and left messages on his cell phone but he still hasn't got back to me,' Graham said as he pushed his empty plate away. 'If he doesn't get back to me tonight I will go and see him tomorrow night.'

Lilly Anne started to stack the empty plates.

'Please let me help you,' Graham said getting to his feet to assist Lilly Anne as she tidied away the remnants of their meal.

The pair worked together in silence as they cleared the dinner table and loaded the dishwasher. Graham felt content and happy in Lilly Anne's company. He hoped tonight wasn't going to be a one-off. He enjoyed spending time with her and hoped that she felt the same way.

'Next time I will make the dinner,' Graham said as they walked down the hall and into the office. 'I have to admit that my culinary talents are quite limited but I do make a very tasty tuna bake.'

'Sounds good to me,' Lilly Anne replied.

Graham looked around the neat, freshly decorated room. Everything was in its place, just like the kitchen. It was obvious that Lilly Anne was very house-proud. Something he liked in a woman. His late wife hadn't once cleaned any rooms of their home. Hired help had taken care of and maintained their five-bedroom villa.

'Is this James?' he asked picking up a small wooden-framed photograph from the desk.

'Yes it is,' Lilly Anne replied not able to meet Graham's eyes. 'That picture was taken about eight months ago. Just a few weeks before he was diagnosed with cancer.'

Graham studied the picture. James was dressed in shorts, T-shirt and designer running shoes. 'I take it he led a very active life.'

'Yes he loved the outdoors. Every day he would get up at six in the morning so that he could have his ten-mile run before going to work.'

'He ran ten miles every day?' Graham said stunned as he placed the picture back on the desk. 'He must have been very fit.'

'He was. He took really good care of his body. He didn't eat fatty foods and never drank alcohol,' she said as she finally met Graham's gaze, her eyes full of sorrow and wet from the tears that were forming. 'He wanted to make sure that he wouldn't prematurely die because of his lifestyle.'

'Lilly Anne, I am so sorry,' Graham said as he made his way towards her. 'I didn't mean to open old wounds.'

'It's okay. I'm fine really,' she said as she wiped away a tears that she couldn't control. 'I will go and make us some coffee.'

Graham watched her dash from the room. The last thing he had wanted to do was upset her.

Ten minutes later Lilly Anne appeared again carrying a tray laden with coffee and cake. Her tears had dried up and her eyes no longer looked puffy and red.

'How do you like your coffee?' she asked as she filled the cups.

'White with one sugar please,' he said. He wanted to ask her if she was all right but thought better of it. It was obvious that she didn't want to speak about what had happened before.

The pair worked together as they sifted through the pile of documents that Bertha had provided. Graham had been right. There wasn't much for them to start with. Only one person had ever seen the creature and had paid for the experience with his life.

'So these are the places that you think the demon could be living,' Lilly Anne said as she stared at a map of Moreno Valley and the surrounding areas. Graham had used a red marker pen to highlight the areas of interest.

'The red marked areas are where the creature has struck. I think these places are the most logical,' he continued pointing to two areas that had been highlighted yellow. 'After all, we have agreed that the creature would be somewhere secluded and remote. Somewhere like one of the mountain ranges in Death Valley...'

Lilly Anne shivered as she imagined herself walking through the valley as the creature looked down at her from a dark, hidden crevice, just waiting for the right time to pounce on her. 'Appropriately named area.'

'Just what I was thinking but it wasn't the name that made me think of looking there. Death Valley is central to all the locations the demon has struck.'

'So when are you thinking of investigating the mountain ranges further?'

'The sooner I speak to Patrick the sooner we can get started. It will take us a few days to cover the entire area. The trench that runs between the two mountain ranges is about one hundred and fifty-six miles long. I plan to take a tent and camping gear so we can stay there until we have exhausted our search of the area.'

‘I don’t think Patrick will like that very much. I don’t see him as an outdoors wilderness type of guy,’ Lilly Anne joked as she thought of Patrick’s perfectly manicured nails.

‘Well, he will just have to get used to the idea. If we want to kill this thing then we have to find it first.’

‘I agree but promise me you’ll not take any risks or get yourself into a life-threatening situation. Some of these mountains look extremely high and dangerous.’

Graham placed a hand on her face and gently rubbed her smooth skin. ‘I already promised that I’ll be careful and I meant what I said.’

‘That was before you showed me where you are going and that you plan to spend the night, or many nights, out in the middle of nowhere. I think the beast has already killed or tried to murder enough innocent people. You are just setting yourself up as a sitting duck.’

‘I know it sounds a really stupid thing to do but I have to do it. I want to find this demon and kill it. I have to know that it is gone from our lives. I hate the thought of that thing watching you and that it might return once your baby is born. I wouldn’t be able to live with myself if I hadn’t tried to stop the evil creature from hurting you again.’

Lilly Anne now realised just how much Graham felt for her. Leaning forward she gently kissed him on the lips. She watched as Graham’s eyes widened with surprise before he gave himself to her and accepted the kiss with his own passionate return.

He held her as tightly to him as her pregnant state would allow as the kiss intensified. Desire and passion consuming him as Lilly Anne wrapped her arms around his neck as the pair continued to share the intimate moment.

As Lilly Anne released him, Graham hoped that he wouldn't see doubt or regret in her big, beautiful, green eyes.

'I hope I didn't take you too much by surprise,' she blushed. 'I don't know what came over me.'

'Yes you did surprise me, but in the best way possible,' he confessed taking hold of one of her hands. 'I know you only lost your husband six months ago but I can't help feeling the way I do. I hope that kiss won't be the last but if you aren't ready to date yet I will understand.'

Lilly Anne squeezed his hand and smiled warmly into his loving eyes. 'I would be lying if I had to say that I don't feel guilt for having feelings for you. Like you said, James hasn't been dead very long, but I do know that he would want me to be happy.'

'So are you saying that you are ready to start a relationship with me?'

Lilly Anne sort of nodded but didn't look completely convinced that she was ready to start dating so soon after the death of her husband. 'As long as we take it slowly. Remember I am due to have this baby in a few weeks. How do I know that you will feel the same way about me when I give birth to James's son?'

Graham gently placed his other hand on Lilly Anne's heavily pregnant abdomen. 'I always wanted children but my wife didn't. She hated the thought that her perfect figure might be ruined.'

'But this child isn't yours,' Lilly Anne said as she bit her lip. She couldn't help thinking that Graham's feelings would be different once she had given birth. What man would want to be saddled with the expense of bringing up another man's child?

‘You have to trust me, Lilly Anne. I know we haven’t known each other very long but I hope by now that you have found me a honourable and trustworthy individual. Please don’t let your doubts about my feelings for the baby be the reason for us to end the relationship before it has even started. Please just give us a chance and when your son is born you will see that my feelings are as strong for you as they are now.’

She knew that she should be careful and guard her heart at a time when she was very vulnerable. If she were to pursue a relationship with Graham she would have to proceed cautiously.

‘Okay let’s give it a go,’ she said smiling into Graham’s happy face. ‘But as I said earlier, let’s take it slowly to begin with.’

‘Agreed,’ Graham said as he got to his feet. ‘And now I think I should be going. You look tired,’ he continued as he helped Lilly Anne from her chair.

‘Will you phone me tomorrow and let me know how Patrick is?’ she enquired as the pair made their way to the front door.

‘I will call you as soon as I have spoken to him,’ he said before kissing her again. ‘Have a good night’s sleep and I will see you soon.’

Lilly Anne watched as he made his way to his car. Once she had waved him off she returned to the office to clear away the coffee cups before heading to bed. She felt her unborn son turn inside her as she started up the stairs to the bedroom.

‘I hope you are feeling as happy as I am,’ she said as she clamped her hands round her stomach. What was she feeling for Graham, was it lust, loneliness or love? It was too early to say and at the moment she was too happy to think about it. It felt good to have a man in her life again, someone that she could look to for support and affection.

'Mommy hasn't felt this good for such a long time,' Lilly Anne said rubbing her pregnant tummy. 'Let's just hope she has made the right decision.'

CHAPTER ELEVEN

March 2014
San Francisco, California

'Hi, sugar, thanks for letting me use the computer on such short notice,' Bertha said as she walked up her neighbour's hallway carrying a plastic container.

'Don't be silly, Bertha. If it weren't for you I would be stuck in this house day and night. Do you know you are the only woman in the street that is crazy enough to want to look after my two little monsters?' Her friend giggled.

'They aren't monsters, they are my two little angels.'

'Are you sure we are talking about the same kids?' her friend joked again, her two brown dimples showing and her long braided hair swaying as she continued to giggle. 'Maybe you would like to adopt them?'

'You know you don't mean that.' Bertha laughed.

'Says who?' she said as her giggling continued. 'Now I have just boiled the kettle so if you want anything to drink just help yourself.'

'And this is for you and the boys,' Bertha said passing the plastic container as she entered her friend's small but compact bedroom that had been made into a makeshift office.

'Bertha, you know you don't have to.' She peeled the lid back. 'Is that blueberry?' She asked, her big brown eyes wide with delight.

'It sure is. Try and save some for the boys this time,' Bertha joked.

'I will try but I'm not making any promises,' she said as she started to leave the room. 'The boys and I won't be back for a few hours so you should get plenty of peace and quiet for your research.'

'You know you don't have to leave,' Bertha said feeling guilty that her friend was leaving the house to allow her to work in privacy.

'Well, if I don't there won't be anything for supper tonight. You will be joining us?' she requested as she selected her coat from the rack in the hallway.

'That would be lovely,' Bertha confessed. She really could do with the company.

'Okay, then I will back by about two thirty,' she said as she looked at her watch. 'See you then.' She waved before she left the house.

'Bye,' Bertha managed to say before the door was shut and she was left alone.

Once she had started up the computer, Bertha opened her purse and got out the folder that contained all her research material. She wheeled the office chair out and took a seat behind the small black ash-effect desk.

She unfolded the glasses that were hanging on a gold-coloured chain around her neck and attached them to her face. With one chubby hand she double clicked the mouse and opened Internet Explorer. Once she had successfully connected she logged into her Hotmail account and checked for any new emails.

There were two emails from individuals that she hadn't before communicated with. Switching on the printer, she printed out the two emails so that she could read them at her leisure when she returned home later.

Once the documents had been stored in her purse, she opened the folder that she had placed on the desk. Taking out the large wad of paper that it contained, she spread the pages out as far as the desk surface would permit.

Finding the page she was looking for, she started typing the website address and waited for the appropriate web page to be displayed. 'The Dark Side of Earth' in large black Gothic writing was displayed across the computer monitor. Entering her login and password she waited for the next page to be loaded.

The site she had entered was a local chat room where people who had encountered different manifestations would come together and talk about their ordeals. Of course some of the users were nothing more than cranks who enjoyed taking the mickey out of the genuine ones.

Bertha scoured the forum for any new names. This was where she had first chatted with Lilly Anne and Juliet. Finding the usual vampire and ghost stories, she logged into another website. This site was where she first found the supernatural information that pointed the death of her husband to the creature from hell.

Taking a deep breath, Bertha shot a quick glance around the room. She was worried about the nature of her research. Never before had she thought of looking for ways to kill the demon. It had never crossed her mind. She had just been relieved to know that she was not to blame for her husband's death.

She searched through the text until she could find the information she was looking for. She wanted to find out more about the only man that had ever witnessed the beast in its true form. Finding the data she was looking for, she read the report over and over again. She hoped that she had maybe missed something the first time but still she couldn't see much that made the incident any different from the others.

Taking off her glasses, Bertha wiped her blurry eyes with her hand. 'Come on, Bertha, there must be something you are missing,' she coaxed herself, hoping it would stop her feeling so negative. 'You know the information you are looking for is right before your eyes.'

Bertha got from her seat and arched her aching back. The small swivel office chair hadn't been designed to take her bulking frame. Staring down at the computer screen she started reading the document again.

February 2nd 2000 10:30 p.m.
Los Angeles
California

The first statement was from twenty-five-year-old Mrs Marie Peterson. The wife of thirty-nine-year-old Carter Peterson, a well-respected, wealthy jeweller from Los Angeles.

My husband and I were returning home from a late dinner date. While driving back from the restaurant we had started arguing. Carter was angry with me because he thought I had had too much to drink and had made a fool of him and myself in front of his guests.

The argument got very heated and Carter abruptly stopped the car and demanded that I got out. When I refused he struck me in the face. Something he had never done before in the five years we have been married.

Shocked and frightened by his out of character behaviour I quickly got out of the car. By then I was very distressed. I ran from the vehicle crying and shouting at Carter as he was chasing me. He looked so mad. I thought he was going to kill me. He grabbed me by the arms and continued to assault me verbally.

He called me a money-grabbing drunken whore and slapped me round the face again. I was so afraid that I tried to calm him down by saying how sorry I was for my behaviour during the evening but he just wouldn't listen. He just kept shouting at me. I then told him I loved him and at first the words seemed to calm him as he stopped laughing and loosened his grip on me. Then he started laughing loudly and pushed me to the ground. I fell hard on the grass verge of the walkway and I think that is how my arm got broken. He then told me he didn't want anything more to do with me and then told me he was filing for divorce.

At that point I was in complete shock. We had been so happily married for years. As I sat crying where I landed I caught something moving in the bushes next to where my husband stood. Then everything went black.

That is the last thing I remember before I fell unconscious. When I came to again the first thing I heard was my husband's screams of terror.

Bertha finished reading the statement not feeling any better. She had read the wife's statement a hundred times. Nothing unusual stood out. She had been possessed by the demon and it was going to consume her soul just like every other victim.

The second recorded statement was that of the late Mr Carter Peterson. Taken a few minutes after the incident. Doctors believe he was delirious when he gave the statement.

My wife and I had been quarrelling. I was very angry and for the first time in my life I actually hit a woman. I couldn't believe what I had done and the anger and shame that I felt for my actions made me react even more bitterly towards my wife.

I remember she was sitting on the ground crying. She was holding her arm. I think it was broken but I am not sure. She had told me she loved me and I had laughed in her face and told her I wanted a divorce.

Just then the bush beside me started to move. At first I thought that a cat or dog was going to appear after having been woken by our heated and loud argument but what appeared was not of this world. It was some kind of spirit, a grey whimsical swirling mass that moved quickly from the bush and into my wife's body.

I didn't really believe what I was seeing until Marie started to convulse. She was now unconscious and her whole body was uncontrollably tossing and turning as if she were having a fit. She started to shout obscenities at me and at that point I realised she had been possessed by the manifestation. I cried out to God for help and trying to bring my wife back I told her how much I loved her and that I wasn't going to let her die.

As soon as I spoke the words the thing that had control of her body quickly left. This time though it wasn't a swirling mass of evil but a real living hideous creature.

Then Mr Peterson had lost consciousness. Less than two hours later he suffered a massive heart attack that brought the premature end of his short life.

Bertha took off her glasses and rubbed the bridge of her nose. The man had seen the beast after it had tried to consume his wife's soul, so why hadn't Juliet seen the creature in its natural form after it had tried to devour little Lennox?

Returning the glasses to her nose she read through Mr Peterson's statement again. The beast had been inside his wife when he had confessed his true, loving feelings for her. Full of excitement, Bertha searched through the documents she had placed on the desk. She wanted to find Juliet's details. She needed to know if the creature had had time to enter little Lennox before Juliet had had time to utter the three little words.

'It didn't get a chance to inhabit little Lennox's body,' Bertha said out loud as she checked through other cases where the intended victim had survived the attack. Every single record was the same. The creature hadn't moved swiftly enough and the words of love had been expressed before it had entered the target body.

'The creature has to be inside the victim when the words are spoken. It cannot cope with the feeling of the individual when they realise that they are truly loved.'

Bertha clapped her hands together in joy. She had found the demon's weak link. 'I have to phone Graham and Lilly Anne,' she said out loud as she rushed as fast as her podgy legs could carry her to the phone in the hallway.

She stopped dead when she reached the icy-cold hallway, the temperature a stark contrast to the warm and cosy office room.

'You are here aren't you?' she whispered, as the happiness vanished from her voice and face.

Taking slow, small steps down the long narrow hallway, Bertha focused her attention on the door at the opposite end, the door that would allow her to escape the closed confines of the house and the unscrupulous venom of the creature.

'I'm not scared of you,' she said, her frightened eyes darting around the walls in front and behind her. 'I know you can't kill me.'

Muttering her prayers under her breath she continued the painstaking slow walk to freedom.

'Going somewhere, Bertha?' a deep, throaty voice bellowed from behind her.

The hairs on the back of her neck stood on end as she felt the cold words that the demon had spoken.

'I told you I am not scared of you. I have God to protect me,' she said frozen to the spot, unsure if she was right and that the evil being couldn't kill her.

'So why are you shaking so much, fatty?' it mocked her. 'You look just as scared as poor Patrick did before I took his soul.'

'You lie!' Bertha shouted as she tried to will her feet into moving again. 'Please protect me, Lord,' she whispered under her breath.

'I'm not lying, you old, ugly hag,' the beast said, the words sounding loudly in her right ear, as if the creature was standing right beside her, its lips skimming her lobe as it continued to poke fun at her.

'And if you and your friends don't stop hunting me, I will pick you all off one by one. Starting with the one that is carrying the baby.'

'You leave Lilly Anne alone!' she shouted turning her head to face where she expected to find the beast standing but instead seeing only the reflection of her frightened, chubby face in the hall mirror.

'She will be the tastiest of all. Not only will her essence taste sweet but the little boy that she carries in her womb will fill me with the greatest pleasure as I rip him apart limb by limb,' it screeched. 'The younger they are the more pain and suffering I can reap from their souls.'

'We won't stop until we have banished you from this world. Your words don't scare me and won't stop any of us from hunting you out until we have destroyed you. And now your visit has proved to me that I am on the right path to finding a way to remove you forever from the earth,' Bertha shouted into the mirror.

'Then prepare to die,' the creature screamed. Its high-pitched spoken words making Bertha cover her ears.

'Go away,' she shouted trying to drown out the demon as she started to run down the hallway to the front door.

As she grappled with the door handle the blood-curdling voice came to a sudden stop.

'Thank you, God,' she whispered as she started to open the front door.

'Don't thank him just yet, Bertha,' the voice spoke again turning her attention back to the hallway behind her. 'He won't be able to save you from what I have planned for you.'

Bertha pulled the front door open just as the mirror in the hallway exploded. Hundreds of tiny shards of glass were thrown through the air at a tremendous speed and became embedded in the opposite wooden stairwell where moments before Bertha had stood.

'Let that be a warning to you,' the malicious voice said. 'Next time I won't miss.'

Opening the door just wide enough so that her bulky body could escape the trappings of the house, Bertha ran out into the garden and fell to her knees on the grass. Tears were now streaming down her face. She brought her hands together and raised them before her face as she started to give thanks to her God.

'Thank you for saving me, my Lord. Please continue to favourably look upon us all as we carry out this dangerous quest. Protect Graham, Lilly Anne, Juliet, Lennox and Patrick.'

Her prayers came to a sudden stop as she got to her feet again. 'Patrick,' she said.

Had the demon been telling the truth, was Patrick dead?

CHAPTER TWELVE

March 2014
Perris, California

David Sanderson got to his feet. Dressed in a black suit, white shirt and black tie he made his way to the pulpit. His highly polished black shoes squeaked as he walked across the white-tiled floor of the church.

'I would like to start by thanking everyone for coming today,' he said once he had arranged his notes.

'My father would feel blessed to know that he had so many dear friends,' David continued. 'Many of you here were his old army buddies and served alongside him in World War II.'

His father had been a captain when the Second World War broke out and he had been posted to Britain in 1942. That was where he had met David's mother. When the war ended 1945 his parents had returned to America and that was where David had been born some forty-four years ago. Like his father, he had opted for a military career but had retired from active duty many years ago because of a recurring back injury.

David ran a nervous hand through his crew cut, grey hair. He still looked every part the air force pilot. The saying was true, you could take the man out of the military but you could never take the military out of the man.

Every chair in the large, white hall had been filled and many more people were standing at the back by the two, large, wooden swing doors. His father had been a very popular man, and had made friends on just about every continent, many of whom had travelled the long distance to be here today to commemorate his life and mourn his death.

David's immediate family occupied the two front rows. His wife and two daughters were seated right in front of his father's white and gold coffin which in military tradition had been draped in the American Stars and Stripes. Standing beside the coffin was a large, mounted picture of his father dressed in a white uniform that was dripping with medals.

David was the eldest of the three brothers and had been nominated by his younger siblings to speak on behalf of the family. The request had come as quite a shock. Everyone in the family knew that David and his father hadn't been the closest for a very long time.

'For more than thirty years he served his country with true courage and conviction.' David watched as many of the old veterans nodded their heads as if confirming what he had just said. 'He loved his time in the army and never once spoke of it as just a job. It was an important part of his life.'

If only the people that were listening to him knew just how much the army had figured in his father's life maybe half the room would be empty. If only he could tell the friends that had congregated here today what Daniel Jamison Sanderson was really like.

'In fact it was my father's love and passion for the army that encouraged my two younger brothers and myself to also choose military careers.'

Yes it was true that his father had wanted his three sons to follow in his footsteps but they hadn't been encouraged, no they had in fact been forced to do so. His brother Billy had only lasted five years in the army before being discharged because of his severe depression that nearly caused him to end his own life. His father had gone mad with rage when the news was broken about Billy's illness. He hadn't cared that Billy had nearly died from unhappiness. All he was concerned about was containing the scandal. To stop his good military reputation from being tarnished by a son who wasn't man enough to be known as a Sanderson.

'He was very proud of our chosen careers and was a tower of strength to my youngest brother during and after the Gulf War,' David continued lying. His father hated the fact the he had chosen to join the air force. He wanted all of his sons to join the army and hoped that David would even consider becoming a marine. So when he had announced that he would be undergoing pilot training this had been the starting point to the demise in the father-son relationship.

'He was a good father, wonderful grandfather and a doting husband. He suffered greatly when my mother passed away and I'm sure if he were here today he would thank you all for your support and kindness when he needed it the most.'

At least the last thing he said was true. His father had loved his mother and had practically become a recluse after her death. He would only accept visits from the family and close friends at the war veteran retirement home. He had moved there shortly after David's mother had passed away as his arthritis made it impossible for him to live alone in the large family home.

Since his move three years ago, David had only visited him a handful of times. The visits had always been strained and one of them would end up starting an argument that would see David leaving even more determined that he wouldn't go to see his father ever again.

David shuffled the notes that lay on the pulpit before him. There wasn't much more to say. 'Seeing as I'm not a man of many words, I would like to end by saying thank you again for coming and look forward to seeing you all at my home at the end of the service for some light refreshment. I would now like to invite Colonel Adam Pritchard to say a few words about my father.'

Taking his seat again, David sat between his loving wife and children and tried to focus on Colonel Pritchard's voice and what he was saying, but it wasn't long before his mind had wandered back to the day of his father's death.

Samantha had talked him into visiting the grumpy old man. He had found his father sitting alone in the rose garden at the back of the home. He was sitting in the now familiar wheelchair, something that he had fought against for months until one day his arthritic legs finally gave in and he could no longer stand unaided. A striped blanket had been draped over his legs and his head was drooped forward as if he were napping.

David stood and stared at his father's large bald spot for a few minutes. He was glad he was asleep. There was no way he was going to wake him up. He knew if he did it would be something else that his father would have to moan about. He would wait another few minutes and if he didn't stir then David would leave.

Turning to leave David was surprised when his father spoke.

'Going so soon, son?' Daniel Sanderson said in a sarcastic voice as he raised his head.

'I thought you were sound asleep. I didn't want to disturb you.'

'I bet,' Daniel said as he wheeled over to where David was standing. 'More like you didn't want to wake me, but we won't dwell on that right now,' he continued as he motioned to a wooden bench next to where David was standing. It appeared his father wanted and expected him to stay.

'So tell me, son, why has it been so long since your last visit? Can't you take constructive criticism from your old dad?' he continued his mockery as he took his black-framed glasses from his shirt pocket and fitted them on to his weary, wrinkled face.

'I have been very busy. I have hardly had time for my own daughters,' David said as he reluctantly took a seat.

'Speaking of the girls, how are they all doing? They don't come to see me very often either.'

'They are really busy at school. Jessica is sitting some important exams at the moment. When they have more time they will visit, but they do send their love,' David lied. The last time David had brought his two daughters they had all left in floods of tears. David still couldn't understand how his wife could be so forgiving and expect him to continue visiting the man who had said such awful things about their children.

'More like I upset them,' Daniel said as he sorted his ruffled blanket. 'I was only telling the truth.'

'Dad, please don't,' David said ready to get to his feet again. 'I didn't come here to argue.' If his father started on again about his daughters, he wouldn't be staying.

When the girls had visited him, Daniel had been in one of his proud military moods. The whole conversation had been centred on his army days. When the conversation had turned to his father's views on today's soldiers it had emerged that he didn't think that women should be allowed to serve their country.

Jessica had told her grandfather that she wanted to follow in her father's footsteps and become a pilot. David had been so proud of her when she had made the announcement. Never once had he pushed his daughters in any career direction and yet here was his oldest daughter full of drive and eagerness, ready to take up the same challenge as her father once had.

Yet David's happiness soon turned to anger when his father hit out at his daughters with the most venomous words he had ever heard. He had pointed at Jessica as he laughed. When he had been able to control his outburst he then told her that she would never be allowed to join the air force. He said that girls were weak and stupid. That all they were fit for was making babies and looking after the home.

At first David had been flabbergasted by his father's words and was just about to retaliate when his father said something he would never forget. Daniel told David's daughters that he wished they were boys. That he was disappointed when his eldest son didn't produce any male offspring to carry on the proud military Sanderson name.

When Jessica and his other daughter had started crying Daniel had told them to go. At that point David's temper had erupted, he let his father know exactly what he thought of him. That day he had vowed he would never visit the old, vindictive pain in the butt again.

'So I take it your wife talked you into coming today?' Daniel said bringing David back from his thoughts.

'No, I thought I would come and see you,' David lied again. 'So how are you keeping, are your legs giving you much bother?'

Daniel placed a misshapen hand on one of his legs. The arthritis was spreading through his entire bone structure and now he was even finding it difficult to hold things. 'They aren't so bad. The docs here look after me well enough.'

'Good I'm glad to hear it.'

'Look, son, I'm actually glad you came,' Daniel said not managing to meet his son's eyes.

'Really?' David answered trying not to sound too surprised.

'The last few weeks the docs here have been sending me to the hospital for tests.'

'What kind of tests?'

'I have been having a lot of bad headaches and I have been passing out. At the hospital they gave me a CAT scan and had themselves a really good look inside my head.'

'And what did they find?' David asked, now slightly concerned for his father's well-being but not enough to look as if he cared.

'They say I've got a brain tumour,' Daniel said as he tugged at his blanket again. 'It's inoperable.'

'So how long do you have?'

'Doctors reckon a couple of months, three at the most.'

David sat in stunned silence. He knew at this point he should be feeling very upset at the thought of losing his father, yet all he felt was sorry for the old man.

'So aren't you going to say anything?' his father asked.

'I don't know what to say,' David replied. 'So how do you feel, are you in any pain?'

Daniel finally met his son's stare. For the first time in his life David was sure he could see a frightened look in his father's eyes. 'Just when the headaches come.'

'So does anyone else in the family know yet?' David wondered if his father had even thought about telling his brothers.

Daniel shook his head. 'No point really, your brothers don't want anything to do with me,' he said as he took off his glasses and rubbed them on his shirt. 'Just like you, they have had enough of my interfering and meddling ways.'

David didn't say anything. His silence let his father know that he agreed with what he had just said.

'As I said before, son, I am glad you came today. There is something I have been meaning to say for a very long time and never actually had the chance to say.'

'And what is that?' David asked unsure where the conversation was going.

'I am very proud of you and what you have achieved in your life. You excelled in the air force and you married a wonderful woman who loves you dearly,' his father said and there appeared to be sincerity in his voice. 'And you also gave me two wonderful granddaughters.'

David couldn't believe what he was hearing. This was the first time in his life that his father had ever praised him.

'I know it's hard to believe what I am saying,' Daniel continued as he rubbed one of his kneecaps and scowled at the arthritic pain. He knew he should be going indoors soon. The dampness in the air would be harmful to his already painful and swollen joints. 'I never have been very good at expressing my true feelings.'

Unable to contain his anger David got to his feet. 'Never good at expressing your true feelings? I find that really hard to believe, Dad. Do you remember the day that Billy returned home after he had been discharged from the army? Do you remember how ill he looked, how painfully thin he had become? He looked like someone that had been held in a concentration camp.'

Daniel lowered his head in shame. 'Yes I remember how he looked. I will never be able to forget that dreadful day.'

'And neither will Billy or myself.' David took a step towards the wheelchair. 'The way you treated him that day. The added anguish and pain that you caused him when he really needed your love and understanding.'

'I know son,' Daniel said raising his head again. His eyes crystallised with tears. 'I shouldn't have been so harsh at the time but I thought it was for the best.'

'For the best! His spirit was already broken and he was on the verge of losing his mind.' Daniel took another step towards the wheelchair. Rage filling his entire body as his six foot tall, powerful frame towered over his father as he cowered where he sat. 'He needed you to understand what he was going through so badly. He wanted you to tell him everything was going to be all right.'

'Okay, so I messed up big time,' his father confessed, covering his worn, old face with his hands as he tried to escape from his son's disapproving stare. 'I thought that if I came down hard on him, treated him as a soldier that required discipline that he would realise that he could fight the depression.'

'Treat him like a soldier. That's right, Dad, the military has always been the solution to all your problems. Yet your stern and harsh treatment didn't work did it?' David said.

'No, it didn't,' Daniel answered in a small voice. He knew that his behaviour towards his son could have been devastating if it hadn't been for David. The day after he had called Billy a failure and thrown him out of his home, David had found him alone and unconscious in his flat. He had taken about twenty painkillers and downed half a bottle of whisky. If David hadn't called in when he did, Billy wouldn't be alive today.

David took his seat again. He knew he would have to try and calm down. 'Well, at least he is okay now. Do you know he has just started a new job?'

'Yes I heard. I'm glad he is on the road to recovery,' Daniel said as he smiled.

'Maybe you can talk to him and your other brother for me. Let them know that I am ill and would like to see them one last time before I go.'

'I will try my best, Dad, but I'm not promising anything.' He knew that Billy had vowed never to have anything to do with his father again.

'Just do your best, son, like you always have.'

'Is there anything else I can do for you?' David asked out of politeness. He still didn't feel overly grieved at knowing his father would be passing away in the very near future.

'Can you bring Samantha and the kids in to see me? I would like to say goodbye and I promise I will behave myself this time.'

'I think there shouldn't be any problems there.'

'Good,' Daniel said as he pulled the blanket up again and tried to secure it more tightly. 'It's getting a bit chilly out here, I had better get back to my room again.'

'Do you want me to help you inside?' David asked as he got to his feet.

'No that's okay, if you could just go and get the nurse for me.'

David headed towards the door that led back into the residential home.

'David, one last thing before you go,' his father's voice came from behind him.

Turning to meet his father's stare David's pity grew. He looked so fragile. He no longer was the proud and strong military man that had ruled his family with an iron fist.

'I love you, son. I really do. Do you think there is any way that maybe one day you could understand that everything I have ever said to you was in your best interest? That I was just trying to help you become a better man?' Daniel dropped his head forward again and started fidgeting with the blanket on his knees. 'Maybe then you could learn to love me, just as much as I love your brothers and you.'

'I will try, Dad. I really will,' David said. He knew his dad was basically pleading for forgiveness, that he now realised that he had made a lot of mistakes in his life. 'I'll go and get the nurse.'

David slowly walked along the long, white corridor to where the nurse station was positioned. He wished he could have told his father that he also loved him, but it just wasn't true.

Catching the eye of a young, dark-haired nurse, he informed her that his father wanted to return to his room. Once she had acknowledged his request, David made his way back to the rose garden. He would go and let his father know that he would be back to visit him in a few days and that he would bring the family.

Taking a step back into the garden, David instantly realised that there was a bitter chill in the air. His father should never have been outside so long, he would really suffer tonight. Very little light was now being fed into the enclosed garden and his father was shrouded in shadow.

'Dad, I will be going now but I will be back tomorrow or the day after,' he said as he made his way towards the wheelchair. His father's head was now bowed, his hands were hanging lifelessly at either side of the chair. The blanket that had been keeping his father's legs warm was now lying on the concrete path.

'Are you okay, Dad?' David asked as his pace picked up as he made his way towards the lifeless form.

Reaching him, David got on his knees and gently shook his father's shoulder. When there was no response he took hold of his father's head with both hands and raised it until he could see his face.

David's body jerked in shock. His father's eyes were wide open, the whites of his eyes prominent against the greyness of his skin. His cheeks and mouth were contorted with pain and a thick stream of blood had started to flow from one of his nostrils.

Releasing his father's head from his grip, David felt for a pulse in one of the lifeless arms. Of course there was nothing. His father was gone, so much for the doctors' prediction of three months.

David took a seat on the bench again, all the while continuing to stare at his dead father. A quick movement at the corner of his eye caught his attention. At first he thought it was the nurse's shadow that was being cast on one of the grey walls, but then he realised that no one had entered the garden.

He continued to watch the shape as it ran from one rose bush to the other, as if cowering and hiding behind the plants. 'Who's there?' David asked, not quite sure as to what he was stupidly calling out to.

The shape was now hiding behind a bush right in front of him. 'You didn't love him. So I took him,' it whispered.

'What did you say?' David said getting to his feet again. 'Whoever you are come out here right now.'

'He's dead because of you,' the evil voice hissed as the bush it hid behind shook violently causing some of the rosebuds and leaves to drop off. 'How will you ever be able to live with what you have done, you murderer?'

'Who is there? Show yourself now,' David ordered in one of his most commanding military voices.

'All he wanted was your forgiveness and love and you wouldn't give them,' the voice continued its jeering. 'You could have prevented his premature death but instead you let him leave this world sad and heartbroken.'

David had heard enough. Whoever was hiding behind the bush must have been listening in on their private conversation. 'You had no right eavesdropping. I am going to report you to the head nurse,' he continued as he started walking towards the bush. 'In fact, I think I will take you along with me, I think you have some explaining to do.'

'Oh I don't think so,' the unseen creature said, stopping David in his tracks. 'You have no idea with who or what you are trifling with.'

Fear engulfed David as he watched the shadowy form emerge from behind the shrub, its tall, grey shape towering head and shoulders above him. Its body mass was at least double that of his own.

'What the hell are you?' David asked in a terrified voice.

'I am the taker of souls, the devourer of the tortured ones,' the faceless shape spoke. 'I came for your father and you gave him willingly.'

'I never gave you anything!' David snapped back at the shadowy shape. He could feel the evil that the creature was manifesting. It chilled him to the bone.

'Yes you did. You wouldn't give him your love. You handed his loveless and broken body to me with open arms. You didn't want him or care for him, you must be happy now that he's finally gone,' the shadowy figure continued its jeering as it pointed a ghostly finger towards him.

David stood fixed to the spot. Never before had he been so frightened. He had served in the air force for years, had seen some really gruesome sights and had evaded death a number of times but never before had he ever been so afraid for his life. He had never believed in ghosts or phantoms but the ghoulish shape that stood before him was definitely not a figment of his imagination.

'Okay, Mr Sanderson, let's get you out of the cold air. You should have been indoors hours ago,' the nurse chirped as she entered the garden, turning David's attention towards her.

'Is everything all right?' the nurse quizzed Daniel as she approached the wheelchair, while taking a sideways glance at David.

David turned back towards where the creature had been looming moments before. He expected the beast to still be standing there, ready to taunt him some more about the death of his father. 'I think my father is dead,' he replied staring at the blank, grey wall.

'I will be back for you later, David,' a familiar, malicious voice said.

David turned to where the voice had come from just in time to see the shadow disappear over the top of the garden wall.

'Did you say something, Mr Sanderson?' the nurse asked him as she touched him on the shoulder, making him jump in surprise.

'Sorry I didn't mean to scare you,' she said as David turned to face her, his eyes full of fear. 'Are you all right?'

'Yes I'm fine thank you,' David said trying to regain his composure. It wasn't the nurse that had put the fear of death in him. If she had witnessed the creature as well, she would have had the same terrified look on her face. 'We had better get my father's body back inside. I'm sure the doctor will want to take a look at him.'

'Now I would like to ask the whole congregation to rise for the final hymn.'

David brought his mind back to the present as he got to his feet to mumble the words of his father's favourite song. He raised an unsteady hand to his forehead and wiped away the beads of sweat that had formed there. It had been nearly a week since he had been in contact with the creature that murdered his father and still now when he thought about what he had seen his skin would go cold, his heart would start pounding and he would start to sweat profusely. The shadowy being had said it would be back for him later but what if it didn't stop there? What if it wanted to take away his precious wife and children?

As the congregation was singing the final verse, David and his family made their way to the chapel doors. Here they would shake all the mourners' hands and thank them for coming. His eyes searched the room for an unfamiliar face. He hoped that the woman he was looking for had made it. He really needed to speak to her. She claimed to be able to answer all his questions about the creature.

A small, roly-poly, ebony-coloured lady was sitting in the very last row of seats next to the door. Dressed in her Sunday best Bertha smiled and nodded to David to let him know she had come.

CHAPTER THIRTEEN

March 2014
Moreno Valley, California

'How is she?' Bertha asked as Graham opened the porch door and allowed her entry into Lilly Anne's home. She was carrying a small bashed brown suitcase in one hand and a large cake box in the other.

Graham took the suitcase and box from Bertha. 'She's sleeping at the moment,' Graham grimly said. 'She hasn't taken the news very well.'

'Is Juliet here?' Bertha enquired as she took off her coat.

'Yes she has been here for about an hour now. She hasn't really stopped crying since she got here. The news has devastated all of us. Have you heard anything about the funeral yet?'

'The service is being held on Friday morning. His mother says that we are all welcome to attend.'

Graham took Bertha's coat and hung it in the closet before escorting her to the lounge. 'You said that some others would be joining us today.'

'Yes, they should be here in about an hour. As long as they don't get lost,' she replied looking down at her watch. 'Juliet, how are you?'

Juliet rose from the cream leather chair and practically ran to the lounge door to give Bertha a huge hug.

'I can't believe it. I just can't believe that he is dead,' she said to Bertha between sobs.

'I know, dear. The news has taken us all by shock,' Bertha replied as Juliet finally released her.

'We all knew he was upset but I just didn't think he would take his own life,' Juliet continued as Bertha led her back to where she was seated before.

'He didn't kill himself,' Bertha said taking a seat beside her on a long, modern, beige-coloured couch.

'What do you mean he didn't kill himself?' Graham asked as he stood before the large ornate fireplace, the focal point for the large cream, beige and gold coordinated room that Lilly Anne had tastefully decorated to a very high standard.

'It was the demon wasn't it?' Lilly Anne said as she stood in the lounge doorway.

'What are you doing up?' Graham half-scolded her. 'You are supposed to be resting.'

Lilly Anne continued to linger in the doorway. The black maternity smock she wore matched the sombre look on her face. 'I couldn't sleep,' she replied making her way into the room. 'It's good to see you, Bertha.'

'And you, Lilly Anne,' Bertha said, her eyes twinkling with tears that she was trying to hold back.

'How do you know it was the creature?' Graham asked.

'I spoke to his mother yesterday. She is in a bad way and blames herself for Patrick's death,' Bertha said as Lilly Anne joined her on the couch. 'She told me that Patrick said some very out of character things before he killed himself.'

'Was she there when he died?' Juliet asked.

Bertha nodded. 'Patrick had gone to see her to ask for her forgiveness. She hated the fact that he was a homosexual.'

'So I take it she didn't want anything to do with him?' Juliet continued her questioning.

'Patrick told her he still loved and cared for her. She told him that she hated him and that she never wanted to see him again.'

'The beast must have been watching and listening,' Graham added.

'It must have been. A few moments later Patrick broke a glass and then started verbally assaulting his mother. His actions and out of character behaviour scared her and she actually feared for her life.'

'Yet we all know she had nothing to worry about,' Graham said with irony. 'The demon didn't want her. It had already taken control of Patrick. It was already feeding on his grief.'

'He then asked her if she would be able to live with herself after his death.'

'Of course the demon had to make sure that his mother took the blame for Patrick's death,' Graham finished his analysis of what had happened.

'How did he die?' Lilly Anne asked. 'It wasn't a slow death was it?'

'No dear, it only took moments. He cut his throat with the broken glass. He severed the main artery and died very quickly.'

Graham took a seat beside Lilly Anne and held her hand tightly as the four friends sat in silence, remembering Patrick.

'I knew that Patrick had been killed by the demon before I went to visit his mother,' Bertha said breaking the silence.

'What do you mean?' Graham quizzed.

'The day after Patrick's death I had an unexpected and unwanted visitor.'

'The demon!' Juliet practically shouted out in fear.

'Yes, it came to warn me. It tried to scare me, it knows about our plans.'

'When was this?' Juliet asked.

'Last Friday afternoon.'

'So why did it take you so long to tell us about Patrick's death?' Graham asked.

'I had to make sure the beast wasn't just trying to scare me off. I didn't get to speak to his mother until yesterday morning. It was the first day since Patrick's death that she had been fit to talk with anyone.'

'Did it harm you in any way?' Graham asked concerned for the old lady.

'No but it made me realise that the information I had found was correct. That now I know how we can make the creature appear in its natural form. That's why it was trying to scare me. It didn't want me to share the information with you all as it knows we are now nearer to finding a way to destroy it.'

'Do you still plan to go ahead with trying to kill it?' Juliet asked.

'Of course,' Bertha said. 'It wants us to be scared. It thinks of us humans as nothing more than cattle waiting to be slaughtered one by one. If we give in to the demon's scare tactics then it will go on killing innocent individuals.'

'Well you can count me out,' Juliet said as the tears continued to flow from her eyes, her pale pink, satin blouse dotted with teardrop stains. 'It knows what we are up to. It has killed Patrick and it has warned you, Bertha. Who's to say it won't be coming after my Lennox next?'

'None of us can say that it won't try to warn you off or scare you next,' Lilly Anne said. 'Then again it may come after me next but that is a chance I am willing to take.'

'Don't you worry about your unborn baby?' Juliet asked.

'Of course I do and that is why I think it is important that we carry out our plan. I don't want to spend the rest of my life looking over my shoulder, all the time wondering if the creature is watching me, waiting for me to slip up so that it can take my baby away.'

Juliet covered her face with her hands and started to sob uncontrollably. 'I can't do it. I'm so scared. I have the same dream every night. The same dream where I tell Lennox I love him but this time I am too late.'

Lilly Anne got up from her seat and manoeuvred her pregnant form on to the arm of the chair that Juliet was sitting in. She placed a supportive arm around one of her newest and dearest friends. 'It must be very hard for you coping with what happened. Until we find and kill this demon I want Lennox and you to come and stay with me.'

Juliet removed her hands from her face. 'We couldn't. You are due to have the baby so soon, I wouldn't want to burden you further.'

'You won't and anyway I want Bertha to stay here as well. I think us girls would be safer in numbers don't you?' she said turning her attention to Graham, her sincere smile lighting up the room and relaxing the atmosphere.

'I agree with Lilly Anne,' Graham said. 'On one condition.'

'And what would that be?' Bertha quizzed.

'That I also stay here. I think you damsels need a strong and handsome man around to be your protecting hero,' he said as he jokingly flexed his biceps.

'You are so modest,' Lilly Anne laughed. 'And I accept the offer. After all, we will need someone to do the cleaning.'

The four friends sat laughing, huddled together as they helped to support one another through what stood ahead. They had known one another for such a short space of time but tragedy had bonded them strongly together.

CHAPTER FOURTEEN

'Everyone, this is David Sanderson,' Bertha said introducing the first of three expected guests.

Graham, Lilly Anne and Juliet exchanged pleasantries with the latest member of their demon-hunting party, trying to make him feel welcome into their exclusive and small group.

'So do you live locally?' Lilly Anne politely asked.

'My family and I live in Perris,' David replied before taking a seat on the couch between Bertha and Juliet. His tall, lean frame towering above the two women that sat on either side of him.

'David lost his father just a few days ago,' Bertha said.

'I'm so sorry to hear that,' Lilly Anne said with feeling.

'So have you all lost someone under the same set of circumstances?' David asked, finding it hard to believe that he was sitting in a room with four strangers trying to find out if a demon had killed their loved ones. If any of his air force buddies could see or hear him now they would think he had lost his marbles and part of him would probably agree with them.

'Most of us have,' Graham answered on behalf of the group. 'Lilly Anne and Bertha both lost their husbands and I lost my wife but Juliet's son had a lucky escape.' Graham thought about mentioning Patrick but then thought against it. The last thing he wanted to do was scare the man.

'I have to admit that I am having a hard time believing that a creature from hell killed my father,' David admitted to the group. 'I don't think my wife and kids would believe me if I told them what I saw that night.'

'It's best you don't tell them anyway,' Graham warned him.

'Why?' David asked looking around the room at the sombre faces.

'This creature is still watching you,' Graham continued. 'Just as it has been watching the rest of us. It knows that we are planning to hunt it out and destroy it and it has let us know that it isn't too pleased by our plans.'

'So in other words me being here could actually put my family at risk?' David said as fear for his wife and children swept through his body.

'They were at risk right from the minute you saw the demon,' Bertha told him. 'This creature wants to watch you and your family being destroyed. It thrives on pain and anguish.'

David sat in silence, his mind recollecting the wicked vision on the night of his father's death. It had killed one member of his family already. There was no way he would allow the demon to harm his wife or daughters.

'Bertha told me that you want to kill this thing. Do you really think that is possible?' David said his voice full of doubt.

'Yes we do,' Graham forcefully answered. 'But first of all we have to find out where this thing is hiding between meals. I have a few suggested areas and was hoping that someone would be willing to accompany me on checking them out.'

He turned and looked directly at Lilly Anne. 'And before you say anything, you are already counted out.'

'I'll go with you,' David said. 'I want this thing out of my life just as much as the rest of you, now that I know my family isn't safe. So where do you think we should be looking?'

'If you want I can show you. I have a map all marked out in Lilly Anne's study,' he said as David got to his feet.

'No time like the present,' David said as the pair made their way out of the lounge.

'So, David, do you know this area very well?' Graham asked as he opened the map and smoothed it out on the desk.

'I know this place like the back of my hand. I was a pilot in the United States Air Force and served at the Moreno Valley base. I have flown over the region of California more times than I can remember.'

'Well, I think that the creature must hide somewhere remote and secluded and we reckon this is where the evil son of a bitch rests between meals.' Graham pointed to Death Valley.

'Good choice,' David said as his eyes wandered around the areas that Graham had marked out. 'It could also be hiding out here,' he said pointing to Mojave National Preserve an area that Graham hadn't thought of. 'If we don't get any luck at Death Valley then I think this area would be worth a look.'

'I don't think we should have too much to worry about finding what we are looking for in Death Valley,' Graham informed him. 'Bertha has been busy researching the area and from what she had found we believe that the beast is hiding somewhere in the valley.'

'What did she find?' David asked, his face full of interest.

'Reports from tourists, rangers and people who live and work in the valley. They have all reported weird and wonderful sightings.'

'Such as?'

'Shapes in the sky, weird animals, ghosts and the usual things that walkers and other outdoor adventurers think they see when they are dehydrated or overtired from pushing themselves to the limit.'

'But what does that have to do with the demon?'

'Other reports have been more interesting to our task,' Graham informed him. 'About fifty per cent of the bizarre reports have been sightings of a grey, dense cloud or mist moving across the valley floor. There have even been a few sightings of a cloaked phantom.'

'So when are you planning on taking a look?' David quizzed.

'How does tomorrow morning sound? Are you up to a camping trip?'

'Fine by me but we will have to go over what kit we will need. I have a four-man tent that's in good condition. Also do you have a pair of good hiking or climbing boots? Trainers and jeans wouldn't be suitable attire. I used to run through the valley as part of my fitness training. It's a very dangerous place if you're an inexperienced climber or poorly equipped.'

Graham could feel himself getting annoyed. David seemed to think that he was some kind of idiot. Of course he was going to be suitably dressed for such a trip. Maybe he hadn't yet worked out the finer details for the planned outing but the desire to find the creature as soon as possible had given him the drive to move ahead quickly with the plan. He was determined to have the creature out of Lilly Anne's life before the baby was born. Their safety was all that mattered to him.

'You look like you are in good enough shape,' David said looking Graham up and down. 'Bring plenty of fluids. If we want to cover as much of the valley as possible in a few days we will have to move quickly and the valley can get very hot at this time of year.'

'I am aware of that,' Graham said, his words deliberate and slow letting David know he didn't need to say any more. 'I have been mountaineering before and I can guarantee that no matter how fast you move I will be able to keep up with you.'

Graham stopped himself from saying any more. He didn't want to sound rude, after all, if the pair got off on the wrong foot it would affect the trip. They needed to be focused on the plan ahead not be at loggerheads over who was the fittest or most knowledgeable about the area.

There was a light rap on the office door before Bertha bounded in with a huge smile on her face. 'The other two visitors are here,' she excitedly said. 'You've got to come and meet them,' she continued with giddiness. 'They are the ones that are going to make it possible.'

'Possible for what?' Graham asked.

Bertha's smile widened. 'To kill the demon.'

CHAPTER FIFTEEN

'Are you sure there isn't another way?' Graham asked Bertha, his uncertainty and sense of impending doom written all over his worried face.

Bertha knew that Tina and Mike would be in danger but their eagerness to help destroy the demon had helped sway her into believing that they could pull off the stunt. 'No this is the only way.'

'So what you are saying is that the only way to get this thing is to allow it to enter one of our bodies?' Graham continued his opposition to the idea.

'My body,' Mike added. 'I am willing to do this and anyway I am the only one who can do it.'

'There must be another way,' Graham said. 'It's just too dangerous. None of us know what effect the demon will have on you. Who's to say that it won't leave you with some sort of physical or mental damage?'

'I know it sounds crazy,' Bertha said and meant it. 'But the only way to get this thing is by forcing it out of someone with words of true love.'

Graham was far from convinced that the suicidal plan had any chance of working. 'I don't mean to be cheeky and I mean no disrespect to you, Tina, but what if you panic and don't say the words in time? By the looks of things you have been through a lot lately. The beast has done a good job in trying to scare you.'

Tina looked down at her bandaged hands. Some of the cuts from the night of the attack had been a lot worse than Mike and her had originally thought. The doctors had worked for hours stitching cuts up and down her hands and arms. She would be permanently scarred, not just emotionally but also physically.

'This thing wants me dead. It told me it would be watching me all the time. I can't sleep at night for fear that I might not wake up the next day,' she said turning her attention to her ever-loving and supportive boyfriend. 'If it wasn't for Mike's love I wouldn't have got through the last few weeks. There is no way I would allow the demon to take him away from me.'

'That's easy to say here and now,' Graham said continuing his argument against Bertha's crazy idea. 'But this thing is going to be a hell of a mad demon when it finds out what we are planning to do. Do you really think the demon will make it easy for us on the night? That it will just roll over and die for us? This thing will not give in without a fight and from what we know about it we are in for a very bloody battle.'

'I know that we are putting Mike and Tina in a lot of danger but there is no other way. Out of all of us only two people have actually survived an attack,' Bertha said as she looked at Juliet's troubled face. 'Little Lennox and Tina.'

Bertha watched as Juliet nodded in agreement.

'There is no way that we can involve an innocent child in our plans even though we know that the love between Juliet and Lennox is one of the most purest forms of love on the earth and probably would be the most repugnant to the demon.'

Bertha got to her feet and stood before the fireplace. She wanted to get the attention of everyone in the room as she made her final plea for support. She hated the thought of putting the teenage couple in jeopardy but she knew that there wasn't another option. Now she had to convince everyone else.

'The only way to kill this thing is through love, true love that is expressed between two human beings. On the night of the attack God blessed Tina and today Mike and her are able to continue to express their love for one another. From what they have told me the attack has made their love blossom and made them more determined to live a full and happy life together.'

'We just got engaged yesterday and plan to get married as soon as possible after we have helped kill the creature.' Mike smiled as he placed a loving arm round Tina.

'That's if you both survive,' Graham scowled, his sobering words putting dampeners on the happy announcement.

'Of course they will. After all, we will all be there to make sure that they do,' Bertha said in a very annoyed voice as she defensively crossed her arms across her chest. 'Can I count on you all to help us?'

'You can count me in.' David quickly answered her question, his military voice commanding everyone's attention. 'I want to help in any way I can to kill this thing.'

'Thank you, David,' Bertha said smiling.

Graham continued to observe the loving young couple. Who was to say that either of them was just pretending to be so in love? Maybe Mike had wanted out of the relationship when the beast had appeared and now felt as though he shouldn't walk out on Tina, as he felt to blame for her injuries.

'I am willing to help as long as I know that Lennox will be safe.' Juliet's words were filled with worry and dread as she thought of facing the creature that wanted her son dead. 'I will send him to his uncle and aunt in Florida. The further away he is the better.'

'What about you Lilly Anne?' Bertha asked.

Lilly Anne rubbed her stomach. Her unborn son was kicking again. She couldn't wait to meet her baby, to hold him in her arms for the first time. Yet if the beast had its way she would soon be dead like Patrick, her and her precious baby.

'No way!' Graham exclaimed, his face full of anger and rage. He couldn't believe that Bertha would expect Lilly Anne to accompany them on their dangerous quest. 'There is no way that Lilly Anne will be there. Have you lost your mind or haven't you noticed that she is heavily pregnant?'

'No I am quite in control of my senses and functions!' Bertha snapped back at Graham, her hands now on her hips. 'We need everyone there. None of us know how powerful the demon will become when it presents itself in its natural form.'

'More the reason for her not to be there!' Graham said, as he got to his feet, ready to challenge Bertha further. 'You're right that none of us have any idea as to what this thing will be capable of when it's vulnerable. Hell! We don't even know that we will be able to destroy it. Remember this thing isn't human. Just because it will be solid doesn't mean that we will be able to kill it.'

'So what are you saying, Graham? Should we just give in now? Not bother hunting it out? Just let it continue to scare us for the rest of our lives?' Bertha shouted back at him as she took a forceful step towards him, her sheer bulking frame a powerful presence as she continued to stand up to him.

'No, Bertha, I am not some yellow-bellied coward. I want to get this thing just as much as you do but I don't want to put innocent lives at risk,' Graham continued his case as he turned to look down on Lilly Anne and her pregnant swelling.

'Right you two I have heard enough!' Lilly Anne exclaimed as she got to her feet. 'Just because I'm pregnant doesn't mean that I can't think for myself,' she continued in a less aggressive voice as she placed a hand on Graham's arm as she tried to defuse the situation. 'Graham, can you give me a hand in the kitchen.'

Graham turned to meet Lilly Anne's eyes, her delicate feminine face a calming influence as guilt replaced anger as he thought about how he had acted. He shouldn't have lost his temper in front of her.

'I think we could all do with a cup of coffee, maybe even something a bit stronger,' Lilly Anne said as she turned to the rest of the guests watching as they all nodded their approval to a break from the argument.

Lilly Anne led Graham to the kitchen and gestured to him to take a seat at the table. 'I know you care for me and are worried about the safety of the baby,' she said as she filled the kettle. 'And I really appreciate it.'

'But,' Graham said as Lilly Anne came to join him at the table.

'I can make my own decisions.'

'I never said you couldn't. I was just so angry at Bertha. She is that hell-bent on killing this thing. Sometimes I think she wanted to get to know us just so she had an army to help fight the demon.'

Lilly Anne reached across the table and took hold of Graham's hands. She allowed him to entwine his fingers with hers. 'I will be going with you.'

'No. Please say you are joking,' Graham said, his shocked and concerned face bringing a fraction of doubt to her decision causing her to look away from his disbelieving eyes. 'I can't bear the thought of you being put in so much danger.'

'But have you considered the other option?' Lilly Anne quizzed him. 'When the creature realises that you are standing outside its lair, armed to the hilt, waiting for it to come out so that you can kill it, are you certain that it will wait around? Has anyone thought that it might flee and go and search out the weak link?'

Graham took in a deep breath of air. The scenario that Lilly Anne had just laid out had not crossed his mind before.

'And who is the weak link?' Lilly Anne said as she continued her assessment of what could happen. 'Me of course, the pregnant woman who has been left all alone to fend for herself.'

The pair continued to sit holding hands. Neither of them cared that the kettle had now boiled and that the guests would probably be wondering where they had got to.

'All right,' Graham conceded. 'But you have to promise me that you will remain at my side the whole time. I don't want you out of my sight for a moment.'

'I promise,' Lilly Anne answered as her eyes locked with Graham's. He cared for her deeply making her feel loved and wanted. She felt a strong connection and bond with Graham, a connection that was just as strong as the one she had had with James.

'Do you two need any help in here?' Bertha enquired from the room entrance.

'Will I tell her?' Graham grinned.

Lilly Anne nodded before releasing his hands so that she could go and make the coffee.

'You have the full support of us both.'

Bertha clasped her hands and closed her eyes in delight. 'That's wonderful,' she said, opening her eyes again, her face beaming as bright as her radiant smile. 'So who would like a slice of my toffee and cream pie?'

CHAPTER SIXTEEN

March 2014
San Francisco, California

'How can I serve you, master?' thirty-nine-year-old Wayne Kilwinnie asked the demon as he kneeled and bowed his head low before his new master. A lover of the black arts and a leading member of the Gog of Magog sect he had long since denounced God, Christ and the Holy Spirit along with all that believed in the Trinity.

'You have finally rid me of my treacherous and unbelieving wife. I am now your humble and most thankful servant,' he continued his exaltations.

For ten years he had been married to the sour-faced hag. Finally he was free of Kerrie's moaning and complaining. He had grown sick of her hysterical outbursts and bad tempered rages but most of all he hated her refusal to leave the church and join him in worshipping the true Lord.

Fearfully unable to look up at the ghostly apparition that stood before him, Wayne continued his worship. 'You have freed me from my unbelieving captor. Now I can worship you freely with the true respect and loyalty you deserve.'

Wayne turned his head to look at the mangled corpse of his wife Kerrie. The bloody pool that she lay in had turned her once beautiful, blonde locks into a crimson red, congealed mass that covered half her face making only one of her wide bloodshot staring eyes visible. Her once bright red lips and rosy complexion were now drained of colour as her ashen skin and icy white lips revealed just how much blood she had lost as the razor wire he had used as a noose had cut through her flesh and bone nearly severing her head.

Just over an hour ago she had been alive and well, scurrying around the kitchen as she prepared another tasteless supper. That was before he put his plan to work. After he had told her he was leaving, she had begged him to stay. She had cried and wailed expressing repulsive words of love. He didn't love her and he had told her so. She had squirmed as he told her of his whores. The women who satisfied his sexual desires in ways she never could.

Then she had just walked from the kitchen to the back garden returning with the wire from the garden shed. She hadn't said a word, her beautiful but loveless face blank as she rigged up the gallows and hung herself right in front of him.

As he watched her standing on the chair in the middle of the kitchen, with the razor wire wrapped tightly around her throat, he could feel the impulse rise inside him. With the first drips of blood from the deep cuts caused as the razor wire cut deeply into her flesh, he knew he couldn't resist any longer. She had put the temptation in front of him, just like Eve had done in the Garden of Eden as she made her husband share in her sin.

By dangling herself before him like a forbidden piece of fruit she was using the same deceitful trick as Eve had done. What man could resist when a woman just laid it out in front of them?

So there had been only one thing for it. After all, wasn't he the descendant of Adam, surely he had inherited the weaker side of his personality that included the desire to kill and maim others.

Besides he felt obliged to help her on her way. He just couldn't let her go without giving her a helping hand and with one swift kick he had knocked the legs from the chair beneath her.

The wire instantly tightened with the jerk of her body as gravity pulled her downwards. Her face turned purple as she tried to pull at the noose as if she was suddenly aware that she was about to die. Her body had vigorously swung and swayed as blood splattered on all the white worktops and walls as she fought for her life, but within a few seconds she was gone. Her hands and legs stopped twitching and her head slumped forward as the last sound of breath was emitted from her body.

He had released the wire that she had attached to the exposed beams of the kitchen ceiling and had laughed loudly as her body came crashing down on to the blood-soaked floor. He had stood and watched as her life-sustaining fluid soaked into her pale pink, jersey dress just as quickly as the blood had left her body. She looked so small and fragile now. No longer the tall, overpowering woman that he had feared for far too long.

He hadn't always found Kerrie to be revolting and loathsome. After all, she was the first woman to find him attractive and overlook his flawed, inherited genes from his short-ass mother's side of the family. Because of his mother's lack in height he also happened to be vertically challenged and by the age of fifteen years he knew that he would never become a famous basketball player.

All through high school he was tormented and bullied because of his less than average height. Being a mere five foot and five inches tall, he had no hope or chance of being picked for any of the cool school teams. Soon he became an outcast and his friends were either geeks or other unfortunate individuals with social, emotional or physical defects that no hip and fashion-conscious teenager would dare include in their social circle.

Then just as he had survived high school and had moved on to college life his hairline started to recede and didn't stop until he was nearly bald and left with only a thin hairline around his ears and the back of his head. By the youthful age of twenty-one he had less hair than his father.

Having sunk very low, manic depression had soon set in as he thought his life was over before it had even begun. That was until he had been invited to join a fraternity. The invite had been the turning point in his life. There he found true friends with whom he could communicate. No one cared about his short legs, shiny bald head or big crooked nose. No one harassed or goaded him. Instead his new friends opened his eyes to the real world, a world where God didn't exist.

Where the heavens were cut off from the earth, just as Wayne had felt for his entire life. After all, if God cared about all his faithful followers then wouldn't he create them all in the same likeness? Wouldn't all men be endowed with the same good looks, great personalities and all the other qualities that women found desirable?

His room-mate had been the first of his new friends to open his eyes to the darker side of his life. This had been at a Ouija board party. Having taken control of the board and the spirits beyond, he had started by asking questions about his future. At first there had been no response and after five or six questions he was starting to doubt that an underworld really existed.

Coaxed to continue he asked the one question that he wanted answered more than anything. Would he ever fall in love and marry?

When the glass suddenly lurched from beneath him, he nearly died from fright and would have stopped meddling with things he knew little about if it was not for the answer. When the eye had finished moving, much to his great joy the word yes had been spelt out. He couldn't believe it. Even for someone as ugly as him, there was a woman waiting to love him.

Not completely satisfied by the answer, he then asked if he was going to marry an attractive female. His great joy was surpassed by elation as he praised the god of the underworld for bringing him such great news. Now though in hindsight he should have checked to see if she would turn into a moody, self-centred cow within just a few years of marriage.

After a few more questions of a sexual and vulgar nature, he finally had the courage to ask the question that had been dogging him all his life. The question that had popped into his mind at just five years of age as he stamped to death a baby bird that had fallen from a tree in his backyard. The one question that in his mind separated the real men from the boys.

Would he ever kill a human being?

Now here he was many years later standing over the very answer to his question.

Stealing another glance at Kerrie between his bowing and worshipping, Wayne knew he had done the right thing by killing her. If he had been a stronger man he would have done her in years ago. Put her out of her misery like any self-respecting man would have, but he had always been weak. A weak-minded fool with no backbone. Someone that had allowed a stupid, hot-headed female to rule him for years. That was until he had found his true calling and the one true Lord.

It had been nearly a year ago. Having finally escaped the office after a long and uneventful day, he had remembered that it was chicken for dinner. He hated chicken, especially the way Kerrie made it, so he decided to stop off at a diner for a quick bite to eat to make sure he didn't go hungry that night.

As he had driven through town, he caught sight of the most wonderful image of his life and the sign he had been waiting for. Standing at an intersection were three individuals dressed in long black robes. He couldn't make out if they were male or female as the tall pointed hoods of the gowns, hung low, shrouding their faces in complete darkness.

As he headed towards them, one stood in the roadside with one hand held out as if commanding him to stop. As he stopped the vehicle, another one approached the car and handed him a leaflet through the open driver's window.

Without saying a word he had taken the leaflet. When he read the contents he couldn't believe it, this had to be fate. He pinched himself several times just to make sure that he was fully awake and not hallucinating.

Parking the car he had run after the three hooded beings. He had waited so long for them and now at last they had found him. He had so many questions to be answered but first of all he had to make sure that they were the ones he had been searching for more than ten years.

As he chased them down the street, he had shouted out to them. 'Does he walk among you?'

His straight to the point question stopped them in their tracks. The tallest of the three turned to face him. 'And whom exactly is the one you are asking of?' the male questioned, his tall menacing frame towering over Wayne as he took a forceful step towards him.

Wayne stopped dead in his tracks. At first he thought he had made a big mistake and for an instant thought about running but his lust and desire for the truth gave him a second wind as he held out the leaflet, pointing at the large bold letters it contained. 'The Lord Beelzebub.'

'And whom would be asking such a question?' the hooded man asked again, his voice strong and compelling making Wayne fearful as his knees started to shake.

'I am one of his humble and loyal servants. For years I have waited for his sign and now I am ready to devote my life to him.'

The two other cloaked companions joined his inquisitor and the three started to whisper between themselves. A few minutes later they had given him directions to an abandoned warehouse where he now regularly met with the other forty-four members of the Gog of Magog Church. Where worship of the Devil was a human being's priority and worldly and material possessions no longer mattered.

Here he found out about Satan and his minions, not just the demons that served him in hell but also the ones that had escaped and were wandering the earth in search of souls.

'So, Wayne, you are ready to do my bidding?' the ghostly apparition asked as it hovered a foot above the floor, its huge height and mass a formidable and scary presence.

'If it will please our Satanic Majesty then I am your willing subject,' Wayne shakily answered, unable to look at the spirit being.

'Our Lord will be very happy with you indeed if you accept the task I have for you. If you do not then I am unsure that you will be able to suffer his wrath.'

Panic filled Wayne. He knew he would have to carry out the task no matter how dangerous or challenging it may be. There was no way he would allow himself to fall out of the favour of his master. 'I will do anything you ask.'

'The Lord will be pleased to hear that. Yet I do not know if you are truly man enough to do my bidding.'

'I am more worthy than you can possibly imagine, please just tell me what to do,' Wayne begged, afraid that the demon might leave and his life might be doomed.

'Are you man enough to kill another human being?' the creature asked.

'Yes I am. If it is what the Lord wants then I can kill one hundred people if required.'

'I am glad you are so eager to please but I only need you to kill three women. All of whom are the most repulsive type of woman, ones that confess to be God-fearing.'

Wayne felt disgusted. He would have no problems in killing more females that were as vile and unrepentant as his wife had been. 'They will be dead by the morning.'

'No, I want you to wait until tomorrow,' the demon commanded. 'Then they will be alone and defenceless. They will not have their weak-minded men around to save them from the justice they deserve.'

CHAPTER SEVENTEEN

March 2014

The sun had barely risen in the sky when David and Graham set off to Death Valley. Lilly Anne and Bertha had prepared enough food to keep a large army of hungry men alive for days.

Dressed in a T-shirt, outdoor adventure combat trousers and climbing boots Graham had kissed Lilly Anne goodbye before bundling his heavy haversack into the back of David's pickup.

'Looks like it's going to be a lovely day,' David said as Graham took a seat beside him in the vehicle.

'Let's hope so,' Graham replied as he stifled a smirk and stopped himself from sarcastically saluting David who was dressed in full military camouflage and army regulation black boots. He must have been up half the night polishing them Graham thought, as he buckled his seat belt.

'Last night I thought more about where we should start looking. We both agree that the creature will want to hide somewhere it won't get disturbed so the valley floor is probably not the place to start looking. Besides from what I've seen of Bertha's research most of the sightings have been in the mountains rather than on the valley floor.'

'So what do you suggest then?'

'I think we should start as far up the mountains as possible. If we start with the Panamint Range we can set up camp at the Mahogany Flat campsite. It's located about eight thousand and two hundred feet up and is the highest camping spot in the range. It's also a great starting point for us reaching Telescope Peak. We can take the truck all the way up there and set up camp before we head out.'

Graham had to agree that the military-minded David was right. 'Sounds like a good plan.'

'I used to take my family there when we went camping. It is one of the more secluded and quieter sites. From there you can take one of the recommended walking routes or if you are more adventurous you can veer from the path and do some real hiking and climbing. The less known routes are also some of the most beautiful as less tourists have trampled the plants and foliage. You get to see Death Valley and the mountains at their most natural.'

'I take it that's what you want us to do.'

David nodded an affirmative. 'We want to start with Telescope Peak. It's the highest peak in the whole of the park. I think we should reach the summit by mid-afternoon if we are quick about setting up. Then it shouldn't be too dark by the time we return to camp. So how was Lilly Anne when you were leaving? She looked pretty worried about us last night when we were discussing the trip.'

'She's a bit upset but knows that this is something we have to do,' Graham answered the question, as his mind was filled with Lilly Anne as she waved goodbye to him.

'Bertha and her have packed enough food and water to last us days. So if you get us lost we shouldn't starve to death,' he joked.

'My wife did the same. Maybe she thinks I am camping out with a whole regiment.'

'Where did you tell her you were going?'

'I said I was going on a hiking trip with some of my old air force buddies. I told her I might not be back for a few days.'

'Was she all right about it? Didn't she suspect you were up to something since you only mentioned it to her a day before you were set to go?' Graham quizzed knowing that most women would be suspicious of the sudden departure.

'No, she's used to it. When I was serving in the air force I would be gone for weeks on end with just a few hours warning,' David said as he turned the vehicle into Death Valley's entrance. 'The road to the campsite is quite rustic so prepare yourself for a bumpy ride.'

David hadn't been joking. The road leading to the campsite was nothing more than a dirt track that would only allow access to high-clearance, four-wheel drive vehicles with powerful engines.

'It's a lovely view,' Graham said taking in the scenery below as the vehicle continued its rocky ride up the mountain.

The sun cast golden and yellow light over the valley floor bringing the landscape to life. With such a gloomy and depressing name Graham found it hard to believe that in such a hot, arid place that plants and vegetation could still flourish.

The road continued to wind ahead of them. The further they climbed the denser the trees became. Forests of juniper, pinyon pine, limber pine and mountain mahogany encircled them as they continued their ascent up the mountain pass, the smells and sounds of wildlife and nature filling the vehicle with a fresh springtime scent that reminded Graham of his childhood and the weekends he had spent with his father and mother at the holiday home in the lush greenery of Kentucky.

'In the winter this area is breathtaking,' David said. 'Because the valley floor is one of the lowest in the western hemisphere and one of the hottest places in the world the daytime temperature is always very high. Yet snow falls on the mountain peaks and turns all this greenery white. You'd think that the valley and mountains were on two different continents as they look as if they are going through two different seasons.'

David brought the truck to a stop in the middle of a small clearing. The campsite wasn't as big as Graham had expected with only ten camping spots at the most available on the whole site.

'This site doesn't see that many visitors,' David said as if reading Graham's mind. 'But it still has everything we need,' he continued, pointing as he spoke. 'Picnic tables, fireplaces and over there you will find the pit toilets.'

Graham helped David pitch the large khaki tent that matched their surroundings, wondering what the hell a pit toilet was, as his mind conjured up images of a large hole in the ground that you had to squat over to relieve your bowels. 'Do you think anyone else will be joining us this evening?' Graham asked as he hammered in a tent peg.

'I don't think so. If it were summertime then we would probably have some company.'

'Probably best that we don't,' Graham said, his grim voice speaking volumes. If they found the demon it might come after them. It would be better if no one else got dragged into the dangerous and scary situation.

Taking his haversack and food supplies from the truck, Graham loaded the items into the tent before laying out his navy blue sleeping bag. He had always hated camping as a kid and wasn't looking forward to spending a few nights in the middle of nowhere with only David and Mother Nature for company.

David had already prepared his side of the tent. His matching khaki sleeping bag and cot had been neatly arranged along with the tin cooking and eating implements that looked as if they had been carefully washed and highly polished ready for the trip.

'Okay, Graham, let's get going.' David popped his head into the tent. 'I think we should take one of the less well-known paths. It will probably be more demanding physically but it should speed up our trip to the summit.'

Getting out of the tent Graham zipped it shut. 'You know the way so lead on,' he said before putting his haversack on to his back that contained enough water and food that would last him the rest of the day. 'Just remember don't get too far ahead. The last thing we want to do is get separated.'

The trail that David had chosen definitely was off the beaten track and not one of the usual routes that the thousands of visitors that visited Death Valley each year would likely use. The thin dusty track led them deep into the mature forests of the mountain range. It wasn't long before a blanket of green obscured the sun and blue sky above.

The further they walked the denser the forest became and the narrower and bumpier the path. Large stones and exposed roots littered the trail making the walk treacherous right from the start.

'If the creature is hiding out this way, I don't think Lilly Anne will be able to join us on the night,' Graham said. There was no way he would allow her to even try to make the dangerous and tiring walk to the summit of the mountain.

Instead he would pack her off to his sister's in Canada. She would be thousands of miles away from the demon and hopefully out of harm's reach.

A chirping of a bird or the rustling of bushes only broke the eerie quiet of the surroundings as a startled animal scurried out of their sight. With each step, Graham felt more and more isolated and more and more vulnerable. Neither David nor himself had come equipped with weapons of any type. They had come to the mountain unarmed on the assumption that the demon couldn't harm them. After all, it only killed people when it had entered their body, when it was consuming the soul.

The hairs on the back of Graham's neck stood on end as a horrible thought crossed his mind. Maybe the demon couldn't get access to their souls but who was to say that it wouldn't try and kill them in a different way? Bertha had said that the creature couldn't harm a human unless it got inside them. Who was to say she was right? After all, her assumptions were based on research material and nothing more. Maybe the creature could enter the body of one of the creatures that inhabited the mountain and possess it so that it could become a killing machine.

'Tell me, David, do any large animals inhabit the forests?' Graham asked trying not to sound anxious.

'Wolves are the biggest beasts you'll find here. Though you aren't likely to come across one. They don't like humans very much,' David replied as he carried on leading the way up the mountain path. 'But in the winter you can hear them howling. It's a bit unnerving the first time you hear them.'

At least it wasn't the winter. Graham felt slightly relieved. Yet he didn't like the fact that such a large mammal lived in the forests, one with big fangs and sharp claws that could easily rip a man to shreds.

A loud rustling from the bushes beside him made him nearly jump out of his shirt. His eyes darted wildly from side to side as he expected to see the swirling venomous mass of the demon or a drooling, hungry wolf waiting to pounce. As his heart raced and his pulse quickened in panic he didn't notice an exposed tree root in the pathway. He tripped over it and was brought crashing to his knees as a startled bird flew from the bush.

'Are you okay?' David said as he turned to find Graham nearly face down in the dirt.

'I'm fine,' Graham said getting to his feet, his face red with embarrassment.

'Do you want to stop for a drink?' David asked. 'We have been walking for more than an hour now.'

'Honestly, I'm fine. I just wasn't paying attention. We really should get on.'

'Yeah, you're right,' David agreed. 'Anyway, the quicker we get up there,' he added pointing to the mountaintop that was barely visible through the dense forest, 'the more likely we are to get back to camp before dark.'

'Let's get cracking then,' Graham said as he dusted his trousers down before getting in step behind David once again. The last thing he wanted was to be wandering around the woods in the dark.

CHAPTER EIGHTEEN

March 2014
Moreno Valley, California

'I wonder how they are getting on,' Lilly Anne said to Bertha as they sat across from one another at the breakfast table. Both were still dressed in their nightwear, Lilly Anne's huge belly covered by a white robe and matching pyjamas, Bertha in a knee-length, tight, doggy-print nightdress that exposed every lump and bump of her bulky figure.

'I wish they would give us a call.' She had gone back to bed for a couple of hours after Graham and David had left, hoping to get some well-needed sleep but she should have known better. She wouldn't be able to get a half decent night's rest until the men had returned unharmed from the dangerous quest.

'They will be fine.' Bertha smiled trying to help ease her mind. 'Don't you be worrying too much. It isn't good for the baby.'

'I know I shouldn't but I can't stop thinking about them.'

'Well you have to try and anyway I think David and Graham are big enough to look after themselves. I don't think either of them would go out of their way to do something stupid that could endanger their lives.'

'True.' Lilly Anne had to agree, but she still felt the pangs of concern pulling at her stomach. She hated not having

Graham around. She had come to rely on him in just a matter of a few weeks and knowing he was out in the middle of nowhere risking his life for her and the baby made her feel even worse. She couldn't wait for him to return safe and sound and back in her arms again.

'So what do you have planned for today?' Bertha asked trying to change the subject.

'Nothing too taxing. This little one is tiring me out.'

'Then what do you say us three girls just have a quiet day in. I thought we could start with baking some cookies followed by an afternoon of sloppy movie watching while we consume the fruits of our labour.'

Lilly Anne smiled. She really enjoyed having Bertha and Juliet staying with her. 'Sounds like a great plan but we will have to wait and see what time Juliet is collecting Lennox.'

'I forgot it was today that the little darling was joining us. Hadn't we better get Juliet up and ready to go?'

'Let her lie for another half an hour. I think she was up half the night with the nightmares again. I heard her pacing the floor at three o'clock, then four o'clock and then she was up again at six.'

'Poor girl,' Bertha said with feeling. 'Sometimes I wish she could go to see a specialist but could you imagine her trying to explain why she was having the bad dreams. They would think she was off her head. They would have her locked up in a loony asylum before she had a chance to prove that she wasn't insane.' Bertha sighed. 'Sometimes I wish more people knew about the demon, then they would understand what it was like to live a life full of terror and paranoia as you wait for the creature to come after you again.'

'Let's try to change the subject,' Lilly Anne said as she got to her feet. 'It just makes me worry more about Graham and David.'

'I'm sorry, Lilly Anne, I should try and stop myself from going off on one,' Bertha chastised herself. 'Let's talk about something on a more positive note,' she continued with a cheeky look on her round face. 'So how are things going with you and Graham?'

Lilly Anne couldn't help herself from turning red. She felt a fluttering in her stomach as she thought about Graham and how much joy he had returned to her life. 'Very well thank you.'

'Is that all you are going to say? I was hoping for a little more detail of the romance.'

Grinning from ear to ear, Lilly Anne returned to the table with a fresh pot of decaffeinated coffee. 'There isn't that much to tell, apart from he is a very good kisser and that he has one of the cutest butts I have ever seen.'

Both women started to laugh, Lilly Anne trying to control her giggling for fear of starting a fit of the hiccups. Bertha on the other hand was the type of woman that loved to express joy and soon the whole house was filled with her deep, hearty laughter.

'So tell me, what's so funny?' Juliet asked as she stood in the kitchen doorway, still dressed in her three-quarter-length, pale pink, floral nightdress. 'You sound like a couple of giggling schoolgirls.'

'If you had heard what we were speaking about you would think that we were a couple of teenagers exchanging details on our latest crushes,' Bertha said.

'Sorry, Juliet, did we wake you?' Lilly Anne asked.

'No, I was already awake. Anyway it was good to hear laughter. It's about time someone had something to feel good about.'

'Do you want some breakfast?' Bertha asked Juliet.

'Not just now thank you, I'm going to take a shower first. I just came down to ask where the fresh towels are kept.'

'You'll find them in the cupboard at the top of the stairs.'

'Thanks. I will be done in about half an hour,' Juliet said before heading back upstairs.

'She looks so tired,' Bertha whispered, for fear that Juliet was still in earshot. 'I think we will have to keep a closer eye on her.'

Lilly Anne was just about to agree when the doorbell rang.

'I'll get it,' Bertha said getting to her feet.

Pouring a fresh cup of coffee Lilly Anne opened the newspaper. She hoped that reading about world events might just help to take her mind off of Graham and the danger he had put himself in.

'Lilly Anne, can you come here?' Bertha called from the open front door.

As Lilly Anne reached the doorway, she had half expected to find a deliveryman wanting a signature for a parcel or letter.

'This is Wayne Kilwinnie. He's just told me that his wife was killed by you-know-who. He was wondering if we could spare him a few minutes as he has lots of questions about what happened to his wife.'

'Can you maybe come back in an hour?' Lilly Anne asked. 'Give us a bit of time to get dressed.'

'Please, I really need to speak to someone now. I am at my wits' end with worry. I just can't stop blaming myself for what happened. Please help me,' Wayne begged and whined, his amateur acting abilities excelling to a new height as he tried to look in pain and anguish at his loss.

'Okay, come in,' Lilly Anne conceded. He looked so upset, how could she turn him away? She felt so sorry for the short man as he stood on her doorstep. He was dressed in creased clothes that looked as if they had been slept in, his skin was pale and his face looked gaunt as if he hadn't eaten in days. It was terrible what grief could do to an individual.

'Thank you,' Wayne said as he entered the house behind the ladies closing the door securely behind him. The last thing he wanted was for them to escape.

'So when did it happen?' Bertha asked as she turned to face Wayne.

'Do you mean when was I finally rid of my bitch of a wife?' Wayne answered as he pulled a long, serrated-edged knife from his jacket pocket. 'Did I forget to mention that I wanted my wife dead and that I got a bit of help from you-know-who,' he sarcastically continued just as Lilly Anne caught sight of the knife.

'Now, ladies, I would like you both to go in the sitting room but first of all call on the other woman that lives with you. I wouldn't like her to miss the party.'

'She isn't in. She left early this morning and won't be back until this evening,' Bertha lied.

'Isn't she the lucky one?'

'What do you want from us?' Lilly Anne asked as she stood arm in arm with Bertha in the middle of the sitting room floor, feeling very worried and uneasy as Wayne's eyes lingered on her pregnant bump.

‘I have a message from my master. I believe you both have met him and that neither of you have shown him the respect and admiration that he deserves.’

‘Are you trying to tell me that you worship the demon?’ Bertha felt appalled and outraged at the horrible little man’s words.

‘No I don’t worship him, but he is my master for the time being. He on the other hand serves the true Lord.’

‘And who the hell would that be?’ Lilly Anne asked. Her voice tinged with anger and dread.

‘Satan,’ Bertha answered for her. ‘This man is nothing more than a Devil worshipper.’

‘Don’t put me down, lady!’ Wayne shouted as he pointed the knife at Bertha’s throat, the tip just about touching her flesh. ‘You have no right to speak to me like that,’ he continued his ranting, his eyes darting around the room furiously. ‘I want both of you over there by the wall.’

Bertha and Lilly Anne did as he commanded as they watched him close the curtains of the large lounge window.

‘So what is the message from your so-called master?’ Bertha asked as she clung tighter to Lilly Anne.

‘He knows what you are up to. What you’ve been doing the last few weeks. He knows all about the plans you are making to try and destroy him.’ Wayne grinned as he passed on the words of the demon. He looked crazy and out of control.

‘So why didn’t he bring his message himself?’ Lilly Anne practically shouted. She was so scared but determined not to show it, yet she knew that she better not push her luck with the madman or her baby’s life might be at risk.

‘He would have loved to have visited you charming ladies,’ Wayne sarcastically replied as he took a seat opposite to where his captives were standing, 'but he had other business to attend to. It seems he has a couple of unwelcome visitors straying too close to his home. He doesn't want to disappoint them when they come knocking.'

'Graham and David,' Lilly Anne whispered as tears started to sting her eyes.

'Oh, are you worried about your man?' Wayne smirked. 'Don't worry too much, my master will look after him.'

'You wicked little man!' Bertha shouted. 'I don't know how any woman could have loved you.'

'Shut your face, you fat bitch!' Wayne shouted as he got to his feet. 'If you must know I am a very desirable man.'

Bertha laughed mockingly. 'And what type of women are into you? Would these be the crazy ones that are part of the sacrilegious sect that you belong to?'

'I am not a member of a sect. I belong to the Gog of Magog Church. The only true religion where the true Lord and his minions are worshipped.'

'You mean Satan and his demons. The ones that were cast out of heaven for their sins.'

Lilly Anne gave Bertha's hand a squeeze. Now wasn't the time for a religious argument. The last thing they needed was to get Wayne more riled.

'I take it you found out about the soul-devouring demon from your pagan sect,' Bertha continued to mock.

'Yes, lady, that's where I found out how to kill my wife. You wouldn't believe how many people I know that have used the demon to rid them of their unwanted partners.'

Bertha was shocked. She wondered just how many more lunatics like Wayne were members of the sect and just how many had access to the demon.

‘Now, ladies, the friendly chit-chat is over. As I told you earlier, I have come to give you and your friends a message,’ Wayne said as he got to his feet and twirled the deadly looking knife between his fingers. ‘Actually I would say it’s more of a message for your friends.’

Bertha and Lilly Anne started taking backwards steps as Wayne advanced towards them, waving the knife before him.

‘So, ladies, who wants to go first and who wants to watch the other one die?’ he asked as their backs pressed hard against the wall.

‘You’ll never get away with this,’ Lilly Anne whispered as she clutched her stomach, her son was kicking her. She knew he could sense her fear.

Wayne licked his lips and looked Lilly Anne up and down, his small beady eyes stopped at her stomach, causing her to cringe as she wondered about the deranged thoughts that were going through his crazed mind.

‘Well, seeing how there has been no offers, I say age before beauty,’ he smirked as he turned his face to Bertha. ‘Any last words, darling?’

Before Bertha had time to speak or spit in his face as she intended, there was a loud crash and Wayne’s legs buckled as he fell to the floor unconscious. Bertha and Lilly Anne stared at Juliet in disbelief. She was wearing nothing more than a shower cap and smile.

‘You’re going to jail, asshole!’ she yelled down at the motionless man that had nearly murdered her friends as she kicked the knife out of his reach.

Looking up again she wondered why Lilly Anne and Bertha were giggling. ‘Sorry about your vase,’ she blushed as she grabbed a cushion to hide her nakedness.

'Don't worry about it,' Lilly Anne said as she took off her robe and gave it to Juliet. 'I am just glad that you heard what was going on.'

'So who is this creep anyway?' she asked as she pulled the wrap round her body.

'We'll explain everything later,' Bertha said as she fixed her eyes on Lilly Anne. 'Are you and the baby okay or do you want to go to the hospital for a check-up? We've all had quite a scare but you and the little one will have been affected worse.'

'We're fine honestly, Bertha.'

'Glad to hear it but now we had better call the police,' she said as her face turned grim. 'I don't want him waking up without some backup.'

CHAPTER NINETEEN

'Why do you think this man wanted to kill you?' the young, fresh-faced police officer asked Lilly Anne.

'I have no idea,' she lied. There was no way she was going to mention that a demon had sent him, if she did she might just end up being carted off to the same asylum that Wayne would no doubt end in.

'Did he ask you for money?' The fair-haired, stick-thin, young man continued his questioning as he checked his notebook. 'Do you think he intended to rob you?'

'I don't know what he wanted. It all happened so fast. One minute we were eating breakfast, the next thing I know is that I am being threatened with a knife.'

'Officer, don't you think we have answered enough questions for the moment?' Bertha butted in. 'Lilly Anne needs a lie-down.'

The policeman thought for a moment before putting his notebook and pen away. 'If I have any other questions I will be back tomorrow. You ladies really had a lucky escape. This creep is wanted for questioning in relation to another murder. We reckon he butchered his wife last night. By the looks of things he's got a real grudge against women in general.'

'Poor woman,' Bertha said shaking her head slowly.

'Yup, you really were lucky, ladies,' the policeman continued, his face full of excitement and inexperience. No doubt this was the first big case he had worked on and he loved every minute of it. Too much maybe, as he continued to divulge sensitive information relating to the case he had against their attacker. 'Seems that Wayne Kilwinnie is a member of some crazy religious sect.'

'What kind of sect?' Bertha asked.

The police officer looked around to see if any of the other officers that had rushed to their aid were in earshot of what he was about to tell them before continuing his story.

'Some church for crazy devil worshippers, I think it was called the Gog of Magog Church or something like that. We are going to check out their headquarters next to see if any of the other members can tell us a bit more about Wayne and what screwy things are going on inside his head.'

Lilly Anne shuddered. If Wayne was part of some sect, did it mean that others might try to finish the job he had been sent to do?

'Are you thinking what I'm thinking?' Juliet whispered to Lilly Anne, her face pale, her eyes frightened.

'Can we go now, officer?' Bertha asked, sensing the heightened tension between her two female companions.

'Yeah, on you go. I don't think there is anything else for the moment.'

Bertha led Juliet and Lilly Anne back into the house. She seated them both in the kitchen and searched the cupboards for a bottle of liquor. Finding a half-full bottle of Scotch whisky, she poured hearty measures into three glasses and took a seat at the table.

'Drink this, it's good for the nerves,' she commanded before downing her whisky in one swift gulp.

'It knew we were alone,' Juliet said as she sipped the warming liquid. 'It knew that we were alone and vulnerable.'

Her eyes darted around the room. 'Is it watching us right now, does it know that we survived the attack?'

'It probably does,' Bertha said solemnly. 'What worries me more is the fact that the demon has followers.'

Lilly Anne nodded in agreement. 'Which means that someone else might be sent.'

'What about Lennox?' Juliet said in a panic. 'What if they go after him next?' She wept, getting to her feet.

'Try not to think like that,' Bertha said in a soothing tone, trying to calm Juliet down.

'How can you say that?' Juliet yelled. 'I have to stop him before he gets on the plane. I have to go to him and make sure he is going to be safe. I can't bear the thought of losing him,' she said as she fled the room in a flood of tears.

'Come back, Juliet,' Bertha shouted after her.

'Leave her. I think it would be best for Juliet if she were with Lennox. She is no use to us here if she can't stop worrying about her son and if I were in her position I would be just as concerned.'

'We need everyone here.'

'Yes we do but Juliet needs Lennox and Lennox needs Juliet.'

'Don't you see that Juliet is doing exactly what the demon wants? He wants her to be afraid. It wants her to run off.'

Lilly Anne felt angry. 'I know how much you want the demon dead but I think Juliet has a right to be with her son. Just because she will not be here to help us destroy the beast, it doesn't make her weak or a coward. In fact, I think she is braver than the rest of us. She's willing to go it alone just to make sure that her son is safe.'

'And what makes you think she will be safer in Florida?'

'For one thing the demon won't see her as a threat. Lennox and Juliet will be safer there.'

Bertha ran a shaky hand through her matted, unkempt, white hair. 'This is my fault. If it hadn't been for me and my meddling none of us would be in any danger.'

'You can't think like that, Bertha. Nobody blames you for what happened today. The demon wants us to start doubting that we are doing the right thing. It wants us to be afraid, so afraid that we might not carry out our plan.'

'Then Juliet should stay.'

'No, I think that she should go. Lennox needs her more than us.'

'I'm glad you understand,' Juliet said as she stood in the kitchen doorway. Her face and eyes were wet. 'I need to be close to my little boy.'

Lilly Anne got to her feet, crossed the room and gave Juliet a heart-warming hug. 'You should go.' She smiled as she gently wiped her friend's cheeks with the back of her hand. 'We will really miss you but we will see you again soon.'

Twenty minutes later, Bertha and Lilly Anne drove Juliet to the airport and waved her off. With heavy hearts and dampened spirits they returned to the house and starting some packing of their own.

With news that there could be other assassins who would be more than willing to finish the job that Wayne had failed to complete, the two women knew they would have to go into hiding. Having left a message on Graham's cell phone they secured the house and headed for a motel on the edge of town. There they would wait until Graham and David returned.

CHAPTER TWENTY

March 2014
Death Valley, California

Graham's legs were close to buckling by the time they had cleared the security of the pine forest that covered most of the mountain. Now the craggy, grey, imposing rock that stood before them seemed much more of a challenge than Graham had originally thought and as he wiped the continual flow of sweat beads from his forehead, he wondered if he was up to completing the trip to the peak.

'Maybe we should take a break,' David said as he turned to take a look at Graham. 'You look like you need one.'

'I'm fine,' Graham lied as male pride kicked in.

'Suit yourself,. David shrugged and started off again.

Graham readjusted the straps of his backpack and started walking again. The rocky path stretched out before him like a winding road of pain and suffering. He could feel the blisters forming on the soles of his feet. Looking down at his dusty and scuffed boots Graham noticed that one of the laces was starting to come loose.

'Wait a sec,' he shouted out to David before bending down to retie the lace.

To do so Graham took off his backpack. He didn't really need to, but he wanted to waste some time, he needed the extra few moments of rest.

David took the spare time to have a drink and wandered down to Graham to offer him some much-needed refreshment. The sun was high in the sky and the temperature soaring, David knew that regular fluid intake would be required to make sure that Graham didn't pass out from dehydration or exhaustion.

'Here have a drink,' David said, passing the water bottle to Graham.

'Thanks,' Graham said, taking the bottle.

Just as he did so his backpack began to slip, rocks and rubble sending it tumbling from the path and down the rock face.

Instinctively Graham took off in pursuit, his mad dash coming as a complete surprise to David.

'Leave it!' David shouted but it was too late.

His advice fell on deaf ears and Graham was already bounding down the mountain forgetting that he had strayed from the path and every foolish step he took was putting his life in serious danger.

By the time Graham realised that he had acted on instinct instead of thinking before making his stupid dash to save a bag, he was at least five hundred feet down the mountain face and now the loose rocks and stones were making it hard for him to slow down, never mind stop.

Digging his heels into the stones, Graham tried to stop his rapid descent. He could hear David shouting out to him but he sounded far off as if they were now miles apart.

Slipping backwards his butt and back hit the ground hard and he pushed his hands into the loose rocks as he tried desperately to stop. Pressing his back hard against the mountain, he gritted his teeth as the rocks dug into his spine and cut into his bare hands. Moments later he came to an abrupt stop, some five hundred and twenty feet from where he had begun.

Graham groaned as he rolled over and tried to get to his feet but his legs wouldn't support him.

'Stay there,' David shouted. 'I'm coming down.'

Graham wanted to throw up. He felt sick to the stomach. What was he thinking? He could have killed himself. Turning over again he took a tentative seat, his aching butt perching on the jagged stones. He felt like a proper fool and he could imagine the lecture he was about to get from David.

'Are you hurt?' David shouted as he slowly made his way towards where Graham lay.

'I'm fine,' Graham lied as he looked around the place he had come to rest in. There seemed to be a dip in the mountain face and there was an old, worn path running around the edge, as if at some time in the past it might have been a route to the top of the mountain.

To the right of Graham, only yards away, was his backpack. Graham smirked. At least something good had come out of his stupidity, his rucksack had survived the fall and he wouldn't go hungry.

Getting to his feet, Graham wandered over to his bag and picked it up. He groaned in pain as he put it back on his shoulders and the heavy sack hit his bruised and scraped spine. Boy was he going to suffer in the morning!

'What the heck?' Graham said as he caught sight of a strange and out of place rock formation, jutting out of the mountain face. It looked wrong, unnatural and kind of man-made and beneath it appeared to be a cave entrance.

'Are you sure you are all right?' David asked, finally reaching Graham. He stopped dead when he caught sight of the cave. 'What have you found?'

'I don't know,' Graham confessed. 'This seems to be an old route to the top,' he said pointing to the old path. 'Doesn't look like it has been used for years.'

'It hasn't,' David informed him. 'I hike here all the time. I've never taken this route. It must have been out of commission for at least twenty years.'

David pulled a map from his backpack and studied it. 'It's not even marked on the map.' He continued to study the map. 'The cave isn't marked either but I didn't think it would be. It doesn't exactly look as if it is an original feature. Someone or something buried their way into the mountain face.'

'Do you think our friend lives here?' Graham asked. There was a slight nervous edge to his voice.

'I don't know,' David said as he tucked the map back into his backpack. 'There's only one way to find out.'

Graham followed David over to the large hole that had been gouged out of the mountain. As they got nearer there seemed to be a change in the atmosphere. It was colder and darker and there was an eerie, creepiness closing in.

'Do you smell that?' Graham asked, covering his mouth and nose. 'What the hell is that?'

David pulled a hanky from his trouser pocket and covered his mouth with it. 'It smells like rotten flesh.'

Flies were swarming near the mouth of the cave, big flies loudly buzzing. They were swarming everywhere and as they got nearer they could see why the insects had been attracted to the cave.

A pile of animal carcasses was heaped at the doorway. They had been skinned and their eyes were missing.

'Jesus Christ!' Graham cursed as he gagged back the urge to throw up.

David on the other hand didn't seem to be concerned by the overpowering stench or the ghastly sight and he moved in for a closer look. He squatted down near the pile of maggot-infested carcasses.

'Don't touch anything,' Graham said, taking a step back as he tried to distance himself from the smell. 'You might catch something.'

Taking a pen from his shirt pocket, David poked at the pile of dead animals.

'They have all had their eyes removed along with the skin and by the looks of things the tongue too.'

'So we can rule out natural causes,' Graham joked sarcastically.

David continued his inspection.

'Are they all animals?' Graham asked.

'I think so,' Graham said as something shiny caught his eye. 'What do we have here?' He pushed the pen deeper into the pile.

The maggots and decomposing organs made a disgusting squishing noise that turned Graham's stomach and he turned away unable to watch what David was doing.

David couldn't believe his eyes and he stumbled backwards in disgust and horror. 'I think we should go.'

'What's wrong?' Graham asked turning to see David's ashen face. 'What did you find?'

'It was a finger,' David said as he hurried back to the path, closely followed by Graham.

'Are you sure?' Graham asked. Fear was now creeping through his body and he quickened his step.

'Positive,' David said pulling a plain, yellow gold wedding band from his pocket.

Before Graham had time to tell David off for taking the ring, the loud buzzing of the flies suddenly stopped. David turned to look at Graham as an eerie silence closed in all around them.

'That can't be good,' Graham said as they both turned to look back at the cave.

A large, black, shadowy mass hovered menacingly in the opening. If they could have seen the demon's eyes they both knew it would have been looking back at them, watching them intently, waiting for the right moment to attack.

'Shit,' Graham cursed. 'It looks like we found its home and I don't think it's too happy about us visiting.'

'I think we had better get out of here,' David said taking some careful backwards steps.

For the first time ever, Graham heard a hint of fear in his voice. 'You don't say.'

Before their eyes the demon changed its form. One moment it was a black, evil-emitting cloud, the next it was some sort of tall creature, completely shrouded in a black hooded cloak, its face hidden.

Graham recognised the change immediately. He remembered how Juliet had described the demon when it had appeared to her.

'My God, it's huge,' Graham gasped as the hooded monster started to advance towards them. He could understand why Juliet had been so afraid.

Before he could say another word David turned on his heels and fled in the opposite direction to the cave. Graham followed suit and the two men ran as fast as they could. They looked like two frightened children, running home to the safety and warmth of their mothers' arms.

David stole a look behind as they followed the old path that Graham had stumbled across when he had fallen. Luckily it was still intact and not as steep as David thought it would be but still they had to watch their step in places as they made their rapid descent.

'It's gaining on us,' David yelled.

'I don't want to know,' Graham shouted back and tried to quicken his pace, his boots were sometimes slipping in the loose shale and he was afraid that he might lose his footing.

'We don't have far to go before we reach the safety of the trees,' David shouted as he pointed ahead of him where the mountainous terrain changed to shrubs, bushes and more importantly tall, lush, green trees that would give them the covering and protection they needed, along with a place to hide. 'I think when we reach the trees we should split up.'

'What!' Graham exclaimed. 'Are you mad?'

'I think it's our only chance of outrunning it,' David said as he turned back. The demon had gained on them again. The tall, cloaked figure with its outstretched talons was maybe three hundred feet away. Soon they would be in grasping range.

David peeled off to the left once they reached the end of the mountain path. Graham knew he had no choice but to go it alone and headed to the right.

'I'll see you at the campsite!' David shouted as he ran off.

'Hopefully,' Graham mumbled to himself. He had no idea where he was going. It seemed to have escaped David's memory that Graham had never set foot in Death Valley until today. The chances of Graham ever finding the campsite were as slim as his chances of outrunning the demon if it had decided to follow him instead of David.

Graham was still running as fast as his legs could carry him. The further he travelled the denser the scenery around him became. Trees and shrubs ripped at his shirt and trousers as he pushed his way through. He could feel twigs and branches digging into his flesh and he knew that if he survived the night, that he would be really sore in the morning.

CHAPTER TWENTY-ONE

March 2014
Perris, California

Bertha and Lilly Anne had booked into a small motel on the edge of Perris. They had opted to share a room for safety reasons and on the second night, after a rather unhealthy and tasteless meal from a nearby diner, they went back to their room and tried to settle down for the night.

They were lucky enough to get a twin room on the ground floor, a basic but clean room with private bathroom, cooler and coffee-making facilities.

Lilly Anne slipped between the sheets of her bed and thought about trying to get some sleep. She was worried about Graham and David. They should have been back yesterday.

'Are you okay?' Bertha asked as she took off her old, tattered dressing gown and got into bed.

'I'm worried about Graham and David. We should have heard from them by now.'

'I'm sure they are fine.'

Lilly Anne wasn't so sure. 'How can you say that with confidence?' she asked. 'You know what that thing is capable of and if they have come across its home, when it's there, goodness knows what it could have done to them.'

'God is with them.'

'Whatever.' She sighed and lay down, pulling the covers up to her chin.

'What do you mean?' Bertha asked. There was a slight hint of annoyance in her voice.

'Nothing.'

'You don't believe in God do you?' she pressed.

'Goodnight, Bertha,' Lilly Anne said as she closed her eyes and hoped she had brought an end to the discussion.

'I understand,' Bertha replied as she switched off the bedside lamp, plummeting the room into darkness. 'You don't want to talk about it.'

Lilly Anne knew that Bertha was trying to get her to open up. The woman was relentless in a gentle kind of way.

'I do believe in God but I don't think he is as caring and merciful as you believe.'

'Why not?'

'Would a kind and loving God allow our friends and family to be murdered by a demon? If he was so concerned about humankind's welfare why didn't he step in and stop it before it could kill anyone?'

Bertha didn't say anything. Instead she turned over on to her side, facing in the opposite direction to Lilly Anne.

'God can't help everyone.'

'Are you trying to tell me that he is selective?' Lilly Anne asked, surprised by Bertha's remark. Maybe her worries and concerns for Graham were starting to affect her but now she didn't feel like giving Bertha any leeway.

'I didn't mean it like that,' Bertha huffed.

'Then what did you mean?' Lilly Anne pushed.

'I mean he can't be everywhere.'

Lilly Anne laughed out loud. She sounded slightly hysterical. 'Are you telling me that our all-powerful Lord, the all-seeing, all-loving being sometimes puts on blinkers and shuts out what really is happening to us mortal, imperfect humans?'

'No I'm not,' Bertha answered defensively. 'All I meant was that God sometimes tests us to see just how strong our faith is. He wants us to prove we are true Christians.'

'Well if that's the case I must now be the best Christian in the world,' Lilly Anne scoffed as she tried to prop her heavily pregnant self up. 'After all, I've had to endure the death of my husband and live through daily fear for my unborn son.'

Bertha didn't reply, she knew that Lilly Anne needed to vent some of her pent-up anxieties.

'Then to cap it all,' Lilly Anne continued as if she had never stopped, 'Graham may be lying somewhere, injured and half dead, and I am supposed to just say, hey, it's okay because God is testing me.'

There was quiet for a few moments. Only the noise of passing cars and trucks broke the tense silence.

'You really like Graham don't you?' Bertha finally spoke. She sat up and switched on the lamp, filling the room with dim light.

'Yes, he is a really nice man and so is David. I just don't want anything to happen to them,' Lilly Anne said as she slowly lowered herself back down again. She knew she couldn't hide her feelings and she wanted to hide herself from Bertha's scrutinising stare.

'I didn't mean that and you know it, Lilly Anne,' Bertha said in a gentle and kind voice. 'You have really strong feelings for Graham, don't you?'

Lilly Anne turned on her side. It was her turn to hide from the awkward conversation. 'I don't know what you are trying to say. We are just getting to know each other at the moment, a full-blown romance couldn't be further from my mind.'

Bertha smiled. She was glad that Lilly Anne could open her heart to another man. She had been through so much. It was nice to see that something good may have come out of something so tragic.

'You do know he feels the same way? We all know he is mad about you and your son and I wish you would see that just like him we are all concerned for the welfare of you both.'

Lilly Anne felt her heart flutter. She liked to hear that someone else had noticed the way Graham looked at her. She knew that Graham hadn't hid his feelings but it was good to hear that Bertha was sympathetic to her fears.

'I'm sorry, Bertha.'

'For what?'

'For taking out my worries on you,' Lilly Anne said as she felt her overwrought emotions get the better of her. 'When I lost James I thought I would be on my own for the rest of my life, then Graham came along and my outlook on life changed. I feel happy again, even with everything that is happening.'

A solitary tear ran down Lilly Anne's face and she tried to wipe it away before Bertha noticed. Her voice was now just above a whisper as she tried to stop herself from sobbing uncontrollably.

'Now,' she whispered. 'Now I may have lost him too.'

Bertha got out of bed. She hated seeing Lilly Anne so upset. It wasn't good for her or the baby. She wanted to say something comforting to help her but she didn't know what. She knew Lilly Anne may be right, David and Graham should have been back by now and she knew if they had come across the demon then there was a chance that they may never return.

The shrill ring of Lilly Anne's mobile made the two women jump. Lilly Anne snatched up the phone.

'Hello.'

'Hi, Lilly Anne, it's me, Graham. Are you and Bertha okay? I just got your message.'

Graham sounded concerned and Lilly Anne could hear David saying something to him. She sighed with relief and she smiled, actually she beamed with happiness. Graham was okay, they were both okay.

'Where have you been?'

'We kind of ran into a bit of bother,' Graham confessed.

'What happened?' Lilly Anne asked as Bertha took a seat beside her on the bed.

'Tell me first of all that you are okay,' Graham said. 'He… he didn't hurt you?'

'No I'm fine. We are all fine, but Juliet has left town for a while. She's gone to her sister's to be with Lennox.'

'That's understandable,' Graham replied. He sounded as if he had calmed down now that he knew that the maniac hadn't harmed her or the baby. 'Why are you still there? You should have gone with her. It isn't safe for you or the baby.'

'We can talk more about that later.' Lilly Anne smiled. She secretly loved the idea that he was worried about her, even though she knew his concerns were justified.

'What happened in Death Valley? What kind of bother did you run into?'

'David and I kind of came across something,' Graham said, looking across at David who was driving. His bottom lip was still bruised and swollen and the scratches on his face and neck made him look like he had been in a fight, one that he hadn't won.

'We found it,' Graham answered bleakly as he held on to the dashboard with his free hand. David was driving like a madman and at a very unsafe speed. He wanted to tell David to slow down but he knew he didn't dare, not with the state he was in. He looked wired, stressed and maybe even a little afraid. Graham had no idea what the demon had done to him but by the way David was acting it was obvious that it had been a very frightening experience.

Graham could hear Lilly Anne's voice. She was asking all kinds of questions about what had happened on the mountain.

'Lilly Anne, I'll be at the motel in the next half an hour. I'll tell you more then.'

Feeling slightly guilty for brushing Lilly Anne off, Graham returned his attention to David. He was starting to really worry about him.

'Are you okay, man?'

'Fine,' David answered abruptly.

'Any reason why you're driving so fast then?'

David didn't answer at first and there were a few moments of awkward silence.

'It could still be after us. I don't want to take any chances.'

'Don't you think if it was still following we would know about it by now?'

David didn't answer and continued to drive at a crazy speed.

'What happened David?' Graham asked concerned. 'What did it do to you?'

'I don't want to talk about it,' David replied. He looked upset and tense.

'Okay, if that's how you feel but can you at least slow down. Your driving is scaring the shit out of me.'

Either Graham's frank words worked or David finally managed to calm down enough to ease up on the accelerator pedal. Slowly he brought the truck to a stop in a quiet, shaded lay-by. The moon was shining brightly allowing them to see up and down the deserted highway.

Bringing the pickup to a full stop, David pulled a packet of crumpled cigarettes from the pocket of his torn, soiled shirt. He offered one to Graham, who declined, before lighting one.

'I didn't know you smoked,' Graham said surprised that the super fit David would have such an unhealthy habit.

'I don't very often.' He took a long drag on the smoke, inhaling deeply. His complexion was grey and he still had that grim look on his face that he had had ever since they had finally found each other. 'I used to smoke like a trooper when I was a kid but I gave them up when I joined up. Now I only have one when I really need it.'

Graham gave David a few minutes breathing space to savour and enjoy what looked like a much-needed cigarette. Something really awful had happened to him when they had been separated. He had been the unlucky one, the fifty-fifty choice that the beast had taken. It had followed him, chased him through the forest for nearly twenty-four hours while Graham had hidden in a bush, like a frightened child, waiting, wondering, hoping and praying that the demon didn't come looking for him. He had secretly hoped that it would pick David and now sitting beside him, looking at his cut, swollen face and scared witless expression, he started to feel guilty for not having been brave enough to go looking for David.

'How long were you hiding?' David asked. He was still looking ahead at the empty, dark road before him.

Graham felt slightly embarrassed. 'A few hours?'

David sighed deeply as he continued to look straight ahead. It was as if he couldn't bear look at Graham, it was as if he was disgusted with him, or at least that was how Graham felt.

'I didn't get the chance to find a hiding place. The minute we separated the demon was on my heels.'

'What did you do?'

'Ran like hell,' David said as he took another cigarette from the packet and lit it. 'I just kept running and running and after half an hour I thought I had finally shaken the bastard off.'

'Had you?'

David laughed dryly and finally turned to look at Graham. His eyes looked a bit wet.

'No. When I stopped running, there seemed to be no sign of it. At first, I thought it had perhaps turned around and gone looking for you.'

'Then what happened?'

'I took a seat. I needed one. I thought maybe I had a bit of time to get my breath back and then I would go looking for you.'

David returned his attention to the road again as he smoked his cigarette. Graham was glad that he was no longer looking at him. David made him feel even more ashamed that he hadn't gone looking for him sooner.

Before Graham could apologise, David continued with his story.

'I sat down on a tree trunk, took out my water and just as I raised the bottle to my mouth I heard it. I heard it breathing, heavy, angry breathing. It was right behind me, its mouth was practically on my neck.'

'Is that when it attacked you?' Graham had wondered how David had got his cuts and bruises.

'It never laid a finger on me,' David said as he touched his swollen lip.

Graham couldn't hide his surprise. 'Then how did you get all the cuts and bruises?'

'If you were chased for hours on end through trees and bushes, I think you would probably end up looking as bad as I do,' David replied sarcastically. 'I fell a few times. I was exhausted, disorientated, confused and frightened. Branches ripped at my face and clothes, my boots were full of stones and I was starting to get a bit delirious from dehydration.'

'I'm really sorry, David. I should have tried to help you sooner.'

David threw the cigarette butt out of the window. 'Don't worry about it. If it hadn't followed me you would be the one sitting here looking like shit.'

'So if it didn't hurt you...' Graham pressed. 'What did it do?'

'I need some air,' David said and opened the truck's door. He got out, leaving the door open and walked to the front of the vehicle.

Graham was starting to worry about David's well-being. He was very upset, distraught and his mental state wasn't at its best. For the first time since they had met, Graham had caught a glimpse of David's vulnerable side, a side that probably wasn't on show very often.

Getting out of the pickup, Graham joined David. It was a cool, moonlit night and Graham shuddered, half from the chill and half from fear. He knew the demon probably wasn't around, but it didn't stop a shiver of worry from running through his entire body.

'We really should get you home,' Graham said in a gentle, reassuring tone. He wanted David to know he was worried about him and that he wanted to help him get over whatever had happened to him.

'I don't want to go home,' David confessed unhappily.

'Why not?' Graham was now confused. All David spoke about was his wife and daughters. It was obvious that he loved them dearly.

'They won't be safe with me around.'

'Why?'

'Because the demon is after me.'

'He's after all of us.'

David laughed sarcastically. He looked exhausted, as if he didn't have any energy left and was now relying on pure adrenaline to keep him standing and awake.

'Remember I said that the demon didn't lay a finger on me?'

'Yeah.'

'Well, it didn't have to. It didn't have to break my bones and bust my head open to inflict injury.'

'What did it do then?'

'It played with my head,' David told him grimly. 'For hours on end it chased me through the forest. I could smell its vile, disgusting breath. It was that close, all the time.'

'What did it say?'

David shook his head, his mouth opened and closed a few times as he struggled to speak. 'It told me in graphic detail how it would kill my family. How it would get into their bodies. How they would die horrendous deaths and how it would happen while I was there. I would be the witness to the torture and pain it inflicted.'

'The demon wants to scare you. It knows we are set on killing it and I think the warning it gave to Bertha and the threats it gave you are signs that it is afraid.'

'Don't be so stupid!' David snapped. 'It's coming for us, for all of us. None of us are safe. If we don't leave it alone we are all going to die.'

'And if we do leave it alone, it's still going to come after us. Are you forgetting the threats it made before we found a way to kill it?'

'They were just threats. Idle threats. It wanted to frighten us. Make us see that if it wanted to kill us it would be able to do so at any time. Are you forgetting what we saw on the mountain? The finger we found?'

Graham sighed. He felt exasperated. First Juliet and now maybe David would be walking away. The group needed him and his knowledge of weapons if they stood any chance of killing the beast.

'So that's it. You are just going to give up?'

David nodded. 'I don't have any choice. If I don't then my family will die.'

'Okay then,' Graham said calmly as he started to head back into the pickup. 'It's your call. I understand completely.'

'No you don't,' David answered angrily. 'I can tell you think I am a coward and I bet you're loving every moment of this.'

Graham was surprised by David's outburst that was now directed towards him. 'What do you mean?' he scowled, a bit annoyed with David's behaviour.

‘Come on,’ David scoffed. ‘I see the way you look at me. The smug smiles, the sideway glances. You think I’m an asshole. A stupid GI Joe that thinks he knows everything. You can’t stand the sight of me.’

‘Come again?’ Graham said, as anger began to pulse through his veins.

David laughed, a hard, long, sarcastic laugh.

‘You’re losing it,’ Graham said as he turned his back on David, deciding the best way to defuse the situation was to walk away without saying another word.

‘What did you say?’ David growled and lunged for Graham.

He grabbed him by the shoulders. Both hands grasping tightly at his flesh as he pulled him back abruptly. Graham spun round with the force and wobbled slightly on his feet as David pushed him up against the hood of the truck, pinning him hard against the metal as he held him there by his shirt.

They were now standing face-to-face, their noses only centimetres apart. David looked mad, his eyes were wide open and the whites of his eyes were glowing brightly in the darkness. Anger and rage were etched into his face and he curled his fist into a ball.

‘I’ve a good mind to knock your smug, smart-mouthed head off!’ he barked into Graham’s face as he raised his arm, his clenched fist was now in line with Graham’s nose.

‘Go on then!’ Graham shouted back. ‘Hit me. Hit me if that will make you feel better!’

David twitched his arm a few times as if he were ready to throw a punch. Their eyes were still locked together. The air was still tense with hostility.

Finally David lowered his arm and let go of Graham. He took a few steps away and turned his back on Graham who was now straightening his shirt.

'I'm sorry,' David mumbled. 'I didn't mean what I said.'

'Don't worry about it,' Graham said. 'But for the record, I don't hate you or dislike you.'

'You don't?' David said without turning round.

'No I don't,' Graham confessed, pleased that David hadn't punched him and that he had calmed down again. 'But you do piss me off sometimes.'

David spun round. 'Why? I have never done anything to you. In fact, since we have met I have done all I can to help you and the others.'

'Exactly,' Graham said bluntly. 'Sometimes you are too helpful, too in your face. Sometimes you make me feel as if we are incapable of doing anything without your help.'

'I see,' David replied sounding deflated, as if his ego had just taken a nasty knock.

Graham felt bad for being so blunt. 'You also piss me off because sometimes you make me look unorganised, unfit and untrained. I suppose you can say that I kind of envy you at times.'

David smirked but didn't say anything.

'So is the male-bonding session over now? Or do we have to hug and say sorry before we can move on with this relationship?'

David laughed and Graham grinned. It looked like something good might actually come out of the last twenty-four horrific hours. A friendship of a kind had been kindled.

'So are you still going to walk away?' Graham asked. The humour had gone and there was no laughter in his voice.

'I don't have a choice.'

'Yes you do.'

'No I don't and don't tell me that you understand. You don't and you can't. You don't have a wife or children.'

'No I don't but it doesn't mean that I don't know how it feels to lose a loved one or to care about someone enough to want to make sure that nothing bad could ever happen to them. You at least have the choice of walking away. Your wife and kids were never involved in any of this until yesterday. They don't even know that a demon killed your father and if you told them they would probably think you were barking mad.'

Graham walked over to where David was standing.

'I, however, don't have the same choice as you. I can't walk away. The people that I care for are in danger every single day that thing gets to keep on breathing.'

'You mean Lilly Anne and her baby?'

'Yes I do and we both know that Lilly Anne shouldn't have to spend every second of every day worrying about what lies ahead for her son.'

David then did something that Graham didn't expect. He broke down. Obviously the last twenty-four hours had been too much for him and now with his spirit broken, his body and ego bruised and his mind in turmoil, he resembled nothing of the strong, composed man that had picked Graham up at Lilly Anne's house just a few days earlier.

Graham didn't know how to react. He hadn't seen it coming. He knew David was upset, but he didn't realise that he was an emotional wreck. He placed a supporting hand on David's shoulder.

'I'm sorry if I upset you.'

'You didn't,' David said as he wiped away the tears. He was obviously embarrassed. 'You're right. We can't just sit around and wait on it coming after us. I know it won't leave my family alone. I know it was just trying to frighten me and to tell the truth it scared the living hell out of me.'

Graham removed his hand. 'That's what it wanted. It knew how to get to you. It knows how to get to all of us.'

Taking the pickup keys from his trouser pocket, David straightened and pulled himself together.

'I think we should get you to the motel. Lilly Anne will be worried sick.'

'What are you going to do?' Graham asked David as they headed back into the truck.

'Me?' he said, as he started the vehicle. 'I'm going home to give my wife and kids a hug. Then I'm going to have a long soak in the tub followed by a good night's sleep.'

'Are you still in?' Graham asked, not sure if he wanted to hear David's answer.

'I'm in,' he replied as the truck headed back out on to the open road. 'Let's kill the bastard.'

CHAPTER TWENTY-TWO

March 2014
Moreno Valley, California

With Graham and David's safe return, Lilly Anne had felt safe enough to return home, for now anyway. Graham was going to be staying with the two women and secretly Lilly Anne was pleased to have him around a bit longer.

Bertha had called everyone in the morning and now Lilly Anne, Graham, David, Tina, Mike and Bertha were sitting in the lounge. Lilly Anne had made coffee and Bertha had been baking all morning and the coffee table was laden with goodies.

Mike was tucking into a hearty slice of chocolate cake. He was oblivious to the fact that his girlfriend was just moving around the sliver she had taken on her plate with her fork. She still had that far-off look in her eyes as if she would never get over the awful night that she and Mike had encountered the demon. She looked thin as if she wasn't eating properly and the dark bags under her eyes and pale complexion were telltale signs of someone suffering from insomnia.

'So you saw it,' Mike said between mouthfuls of cake and coffee.

'We saw it all right,' Graham replied.

'Looks like you did more than just see it,' Tina said in a quiet voice as she looked at David's cut and bruised face. She was seated on the floor next to Mike's feet. Her complexion was so pale and she looked so small and fragile that she reminded Lilly Anne of a delicate china doll.

'It didn't like our visit,' Graham confessed. 'It chased David. Threatened him and his family.'

'It's a wonder you escaped alive,' Tina said as she put her plate on the table. She hadn't eaten a morsel and Lilly Anne was starting to worry about her frame of mind.

'It didn't hurt us, if that's what you are wondering,' David said. 'I got these cuts from falling down on the hard ground. It can't hurt you.'

'Are you starting to have doubts?' Bertha asked Tina. 'Are you sure you want to go ahead with the plan?'

Tina looked around the room. All eyes were on her.

'Tina, can you help me in the kitchen,' Lilly Anne asked, getting to her feet.

The look of relief on Tina's face was evident to all as she quickly made her exit without answering the question.

'I thought you needed some space,' Lilly Anne said as she refilled the empty kettle.

'Thanks,' Tina said as she took a seat and rested her still sore, bandaged hands on the table. She looked pale, her facial features gaunt as if she hadn't been eating or sleeping properly.

Poor kid, Lilly Anne thought. 'How are your hands?'

'They are still sore,' Tina said sadly. 'I haven't picked up a paintbrush since, since...' She couldn't bring herself to say anything more about that terrible night.

Lilly Anne took a seat at the table beside Tina. She wanted to give the poor girl a hug. She knew how difficult it was for her. Something wickedly evil had tried to kill her and the only person she could confide in, express her fears to, was her boyfriend, a young man who probably just like every young man of his age wouldn't know what to say or do to help her feel better and get over what had happened.

'You will soon. You have to have faith.'

Tina looked down at her bandaged hands. 'I hope so. I don't know what I would do if could never paint again. It's the only thing I'm good at.'

'Mike told me that you are very gifted. Maybe one day soon you can paint me a picture for the nursery.'

Tina smiled. It was the first time Lilly Anne had seen her look something other than sombre and sad. 'I'd like that.'

Now that she had made a small but significant connection with Tina, Lilly Anne decided to press her for an answer to the question she had dodged earlier.

'Are you having doubts about the plan?'

Tina was slightly taken aback by the question and her smile instantly vanished. 'Aren't you?' she asked.

Lilly Anne shook her head. 'No.'

'Why not?'

'Because I know we have to kill it.'

'But you nearly died. You and your unborn baby, Bertha and Juliet could have been butchered to death by some maniac because of our plan.'

'I know, but I wasn't.'

'But you could have been. You were lucky that time but you don't know what the demon has planned for you now.'

'I know I'm in harm's way,' Lilly Anne confessed, 'but I don't want to live the rest of my life in fear and I don't want my baby to be born into that fear.'

Tina didn't look convinced. 'I don't know.'

'Think about it, Tina, before you make a decision,' Lilly Anne said gently as she got to her feet. 'None of us know what that thing has in store for us. We are all in this together and we are all here for each other. None of us will let anything happen to you, but if you are still unconvinced about your safety then don't go ahead with it. We will all understand.'

Lilly Anne started to head out of the kitchen.

'Is that the vase?' Tina asked.

At first Lilly Anne was confused by the question, then she realised what Tina was speaking about. She turned to look at the misshapen, broken vase that sat on the end of the kitchen counter. It was the vase Juliet had used to knock out the guy that had been sent to kill them. Graham had cleaned up the broken ceramic pieces the night they had returned home and when Lilly Anne had woken in the morning he had glued it back together.

'Yes it is.'

'I'm surprised you kept it,' Tina said, twisting her face in disgust at the sight of the cracked, broken vase. 'I would have thrown it out. I wouldn't want it in the house to remind me of what could have happened.'

'I don't see it like that.' Lilly Anne smiled as she looked at the vase. 'Of course it reminds me of what happened. It also reminds me of Juliet's strength and Bertha's resilience. None of us gave up that day. We were all determined to not let the demon win and it didn't.'

Lilly Anne walked over to the vase and gently picked it up. Tina watched her as she cradled the broken vase as if it were a priceless work of art.

'Do you know what else I see when I look at this vase?' Lilly Anne said, turning to look at Tina. 'It reminds me that the demon can be beaten. I think it's scared. I think it sent that crazy SOB because it knows we can kill it. We are on to something with our plan and it will use every evil force and power it has to try and stop us from going up against it.'

Tina didn't say anything and turned her stare from Lilly Anne. Her eyes looked wet and she looked slightly ashamed as if she felt she should be stronger.

Lilly Anne gently put the vase back on the counter. 'I had better go back and see if anyone needs a refill. Take a minute or two if you need it.'

Leaving Tina sitting in the kitchen, Lilly Anne headed back to the sitting room.

'Graham, David, can I speak to you.'

She signalled to them to come out of the room. No one else seemed to wonder why she needed a moment alone with the two men, and Lilly Anne was glad that there had been no funny looks or wondering stares.

'I think we have a problem,' she quietly said as they stood in the hallway. 'I don't think Tina is emotionally stable enough to go ahead with our plan. I think we will have to find another way.'

Graham sighed and leaned against the wall. He looked slightly annoyed. 'Now what do we do?'

'I don't know,' Lilly Anne said more quietly, she could see Tina getting up from the table. 'We will need to speak to Bertha later and find out if there is anyone else that she knows that might want to get involved.'

'What are you talking about?' Tina asked as she stood behind them.

'Nothing that you need worry about,' David said, trying to smile and look sincere.

'You were discussing me, weren't you?' Tina quizzed.

'Yes we were,' Lilly Anne confessed. She knew there was no point in lying to her. 'I know you are having doubts about helping us with the plan and knowing that I don't think it would be safe for you to go up against the demon. It would be dangerous for you, Mike and the rest of us.'

Tina walked to the sitting room door and looked in. Mike was telling Bertha a funny high school story. Bertha was giggling and enjoying his company. To an onlooker the scene would look strange, maybe even weird. Who would believe that an elderly lady and a young man from completely different backgrounds and communities would become such good friends? It was a surreal image. It was just a pity that it had been such horrific, tragic events that had brought them together.

She continued to watch Mike for a few more seconds. He was so handsome. She loved the way he smiled and the way he could light up the room with his funny, comical stories and jokes. When she was down he was so good at making her feel better – usually.

'Shouldn't it be my decision?' Tina asked turning her attention back to them.

'What are you saying?' Graham quizzed.

'I'm saying I still want to go ahead with the plan. Yes, Lilly Anne is right I am scared. I'm scared that Mike might be hurt or that it will go crazy and kill him before we can do anything to help him. I also worry about the rest of us. I also think that we are so wrapped up in being successful that we aren't really thinking about the real danger.'

Lilly Anne, David and Graham didn't say anything, they let Tina continue, knowing deep down that she was right. Mike and Bertha had heard Tina and the others talking in the hallway and had come to the doorway to hear what was being said.

'I think we have to take a step back for a minute and really, really think about what we are going up against.'

'We know what we are fighting,' Graham said.

'I know we do, and we know what it's capable of. Look at David's face,' Tina said turning to look at him, everyone else following her lead.

David grimaced. He didn't want to be put in the spotlight.

'I know you say it can't hurt us but David still got injured.'

'I got these bruises and cuts from falling down. The demon didn't lay a finger on me.'

'I know that.' Tina sighed, realising that she wasn't getting her point across as well as she wanted. 'But you fell down because it was chasing you and by the sounds of things it ran you ragged. It ran you all over the mountain and I think you are lucky it didn't run you right off a cliff.'

Nobody said anything. Graham had originally thought that Tina just needed to vent her fears and worries and that she needed someone to listen to her. Now he was starting to realise that she had a very valid point.

'I agree with Tina,' Graham chipped in. Turning to look at Lilly Anne while fear rose in his throat as a nightmare image popped into his mind. He could imagine the demon turning on Lilly Anne, chasing her through the forest as it had David. Her dress torn, her face and legs scratched and bruised, her eyes wet and full of fear. Her hands clasping her pregnant belly as she tried to save her unborn child from a grim and horrid death.

'We can't take any chances. We have to make our safety the priority,' he continued as he removed the horrid image from his mind. 'There is no point in us hunting this thing out, taking it on when there is a chance that some of us won't make it safely back home.'

Everyone stood in the hallway. They all wore the same grim, perplexed expression.

'We had better revise our plans then,' David said, breaking the silence.

A loud knock on the front door made Bertha and Lilly Anne jump. Lilly Anne turned to Graham. He could see the fear in her eyes. She was worried it might be another of the demon's loyal servants. Another brainwashed maniac sent to kill them all.

'I'll get it,' Graham said, gently placing a hand on the small of Lilly Anne's back as if to let her know that he wasn't going to let anything happen to her or the baby.

Graham opened the door as all looked on in the background.

'Hi all.' Juliet smiled as she walked over the threshold. 'Is this the welcoming committee?'

CHAPTER TWENTY-THREE

'You're a sight for sore eyes.' Bertha beamed and hugged Juliet fiercely.

Everyone returned to the sitting room except Graham and David. Graham had taken Juliet's suitcase upstairs and was now on his way back down to meet David in the study. They had a new plan to work on.

Juliet took a seat between Bertha and Lilly Anne.

'I didn't think we would be seeing you for a while,' Mike said, returning to his seat. 'Bertha told us you had left town.'

'I didn't intend coming back until you had taken care of...' she looked around the room as if she were expecting the demon to jump out from behind one of the seats, 'you-know-who, but after a few days I managed to calm myself down enough to know that I was being selfish and that my place was back here helping the rest of you.'

'What about Lennox? How is he?'

'He's fine. Loving staying with his cousins. He didn't even mind me going away again.'

'Does he still speak about what happened?' Bertha asked.

'He hasn't mentioned the demon once. It's as if it never happened. At least he is young enough to put that awful day behind him. He seems to be back to his old self. He's a fun-loving, happy little boy again.'

'Are you going to bring him back here?'

Juliet looked slightly upset, as if she had some bad news to break. 'I'm afraid that this will be my last trip to Moreno Valley and Perris for a while.' She looked around the room at the people she classed as friends. Good friends, the type she knew she could rely on. She was really going to miss them. 'I'm selling up and moving in with my sister, I want Lennox to grow up with his cousins.'

Lilly Anne and Bertha couldn't hide their sadness at the news but they both understood that Juliet had to put Lennox's welfare first.

'Just promise me that you will come back and visit us.' Lilly Anne smiled.

'Of course I will,' she beamed, glad that they were happy for her.

'So what have I missed?' she asked taking a freshly poured cup of steaming hot coffee from Lilly Anne. 'I see David has been in the wars.'

'David and Graham have found where the demon lives.'

Juliet's eyes widened with fear. 'So when do we go after it?'

'The day after tomorrow,' David announced from the doorway.

'That was quick,' Lilly Anne said, surprised that the men were only away for a few minutes.

'It didn't take much to see where the plan was flawed. Tactically we are strong. Defensively we were weak.'

Graham and David carried a large, grey, metal container into the sitting room and sat it on the floor in front of the fireplace.

'So what are we going to do?' Bertha asked, her eyes transfixed on the unopened box.

David turned to Graham. 'Do you want to explain the plan?'

'No,' Graham said. 'You know what you're talking about. You do it.'

David walked over to the fireplace and took centre stage. He had everyone's attention and he could see a hint of fear and excitement in all of their faces. None of them knew what was going to happen in two days' time. Nobody knew what form the demon would take. There was no idea of how it would react or if it would be easy to destroy. All David knew was that he had to make sure that they were armed to the hilt and that he could provide the safety and protection they would need. After all, none of them were soldiers and more than half of them were women, one of which was a senior and another heavily pregnant.

'We have decided the best place to call this thing out would be at the campsite. During the week the site is usually empty but if anyone comes along, Graham and I will be dressed as rangers and we will stop anyone from camping there for the night.'

'Good idea,' Lilly Anne said. 'We don't want any more innocent people involved.'

Juliet giggled. 'I like a man in uniform. I can't wait to see you two all dressed up.'

David ignored her comment. He didn't think it was the time for jokes. 'I have borrowed a generator and four high-powered lights from a friend of mine. They should be bright enough for us, but not too bright as to attract unwanted attention.'

Mike nodded. 'We don't want any real rangers turning up.'

'Exactly,' David continued. 'As for firepower and weapons…'

'Are you giving us guns?' Juliet asked. She looked worried. 'I don't know how to handle a gun. I don't really want one.'

'If you let David finish,' Graham intervened before anyone else asked a question.

'There will only be two guns. I will of course have one and Graham will have the other.'

'What about me?' Mike asked. He didn't look pleased about being left out.

'I think you will be rather busy with something else,' David said.

He looked at Mike. He hoped he would get the point as to why he didn't think it would be practical for him to be armed with a deadly weapon. Once Mike and Tina had released the beast, there was a chance that Mike might be incapacitated for a while. His gun would be unguarded and David didn't want to think about what might happen if the demon got its evil hands on it.

Mike didn't reply. He just nodded. The look in his big, boyish eyes revealed his understanding.

David got down on his knees and undid the big box. The hinges creaked as the lid opened and he reached inside to pull something out.

'Tina,' he said getting back to his feet as he turned his attention to the young, worried-looking woman. 'This is for you.'

He handed her a long-handled, serrated hunting knife. It looked mean. Reluctantly Tina took it by the handle. It was still in the sheath.

'I don't really want to carry a weapon,' she said, looking up at David with her big brown, worried eyes. 'Please don't make me take this.'

'It's not just for your protection,' Graham said, his tone gentle and understanding. 'You will have to protect Mike.'

'Oh,' was all she said and placed the knife on her lap.

'Bertha,' David said, delving back into the weapons box. 'This is for you.'

Taking the baseball bat from David, Bertha smiled.

'I used to keep one of these under my bed,' she informed them. 'For my own safety.'

Lilly Anne felt sorry for Bertha. The poor, old, kind-hearted lady that she had grown to love as she would a grandma had lived a hard and unhappy life. Once the demon was destroyed she wasn't going to let her go back to San Francisco, she was going to ask her to stay on in Moreno Valley and help her with the baby.

'Juliet,' David continued as he rummaged in the box. 'Have you ever used an axe before?'

'Yes,' she said. 'But only to chop wood.'

'Good,' David said and handed her a long, gleaming new axe. The blade looked razor sharp and the head gleamed and glimmered with evil intent. David had modified the shaft. He had made it lighter so that the tall and slender-looking Juliet could wield it easily.

'This is light,' Juliet said surprised as she held it in both hands.

'We will also be armed with two nets, three bear traps and six grenades.'

'Grenades?' Bertha said, visibly shocked.

'Yes,' David said turning to her and the others. 'Hopefully we won't need them. I'm taking them as backup. Just in case things get out of control.'

'What about me?' Lilly Anne asked. 'Don't I get a weapon?'

Graham turned to look at Lilly Anne. While David had been handing out the weapons, he had been leaning on the fireplace. Now he straightened up. He wasn't happy with the idea of Lilly Anne being armed. In fact, he wasn't happy with her going along with them to the campsite. If he had his way she would be shipped off to one of her relatives in Canada until it was safe for her to return again.

David turned to look at Graham. He could feel the tension rising in the room. He knew Lilly Anne wasn't going to be happy with the decision that they had made and there was no way he was going to be the one to tell her that she wasn't going to be tooled up like the rest of them.

'We didn't think it would be right for you to be armed.' Graham paused for a moment. He could see Lilly Anne's expression change. 'Not in your condition.'

The displeasure Lilly Anne felt was visible to all. 'My condition?' she said coolly. 'You are telling me that because I am pregnant I should be left defenceless?'

'You won't be defenceless,' Graham replied. He didn't want her all wound up. He knew if she was upset that the baby would also be upset. 'I'll be with you the whole time. I won't let anything happen to you.'

Lilly Anne was touched by his words. She liked the fact that he would be looking out for her and her baby but she still wasn't happy. 'I'm glad and thankful that you have my best interests at heart,' she said, 'but what happens if things do get out of control? What if you can't stay with me?'

David looked at Graham again. He had argued the same point with Graham when they had been making the final plans. 'She's right.'

'I know she's right,' Graham said, in a slightly cutting tone. 'Give her a weapon.'

Graham walked out of the room. He didn't want to be there to see Lilly Anne being handed a gun or any other type of weapon. It just didn't seem right.

David rummaged in the box again. He turned to look at Lilly Anne.

'Are you completely sure about this?' he asked.

Lilly Anne nodded.

David handed her a long-handled knife, much like the one that he had given to Tina. Lilly Anne gently took it from his outstretched hand.

'Thank you,' she said as she put it on the floor next to her feet.

'Now it would be best to discuss the actual plan and each person's involvement,' David said as he rolled out a large sheet of paper that he had also taken from the box. He placed it on the floor in front of the fireplace. 'I had better go and get Graham.'

Lilly Anne got to her feet. 'I'll get him.'

She headed out of the sitting room before anyone could object. She looked down towards the kitchen and noticed that the door leading to the garden was open. Obviously Graham was outside.

'David needs you,' she said as she stepped out into the yard.

Graham was seated on a wooden bench by the door. His expression was grim. He looked unhappy and slightly annoyed.

Lilly Anne took a seat beside him and for a few awkward moments neither of them spoke.

'Please don't be mad with me,' Lilly Anne said. Her voice was soft and soothing.

'I'm not mad with you,' Graham replied, turning to look at her pretty face. 'I'm mad with myself.'

Lilly Anne was surprised at his confession. 'Why?'

Graham didn't say anything for a few moments. Instead he continued to stare into her eyes as if her beauty transfixed him.

'Because if I had been a real man I would have taken care of the son of a bitch when I had the chance instead of running away like a coward.'

Lilly Anne was confused. What was he talking about?

'When David and I were on the mountain we should have taken the demon out. Then you and your son would be safe and none of us would have to put our lives in danger just to finally get peace of mind.'

Lilly Anne reached out and touched Graham's hand. A surge of sexual chemistry passed from her body to his and Graham knew there and then that he wanted to spend the rest of his life with her. She was perfect, beautiful, clever, sweet and strong. She was going to be a wonderful mother.

Graham released his hand from hers and in one fluid movement he had her embraced in his arms. He pulled her close and he could smell her perfume. It smelt divine. He nestled his face on her head, his lips skimming her forehead and he longed for her to look up so that he could kiss her on the lips.

Emotions were bubbling up inside Lilly Anne, happy, loving, passion-fuelled feelings that were being stimulated by

Graham's warmth and openness at displaying his attraction for her.

'Promise me one thing,' Graham murmured.

'What is it?'

'Promise me that you won't leave my side, that when we go up against the demon that you will let me protect you. I need to know that you will let me look after you.'

'I promise,' Lilly Anne whispered as she buried her head further into Graham's chest. She didn't want to move, she didn't want the moment to end but she knew that soon they would have to let go of one another and go back to the others.

Someone coughed.

David was standing in the doorway. He looked slightly embarrassed as he awkwardly invaded their moment of privacy.

'We're coming.' Graham sighed as he released Lilly Anne. He noticed that she had turned red and was trying to avert her eyes from David as she got to her feet and hurried past him into the house.

'That looked cosy,' he smirked, knowing that he was making Graham feel uncomfortable.

'It was,' Graham said as he too quickly hurried into the house before David could ask him any awkward questions.

CHAPTER TWENTY-FOUR

Everyone was back in the sitting room. Lilly Anne had made fresh coffee and Juliet had made sandwiches. It was now late in the afternoon and everyone was starting to look a bit uneasy, fidgety and tired. Graham was now seated on the floor next to Lilly Anne's feet and David was about to explain the plan.

'As I said earlier, I have four lights that are powered by generators. These will be positioned at each corner of the clearing.' He pointed to a square area that he had marked out on the map. It ran around the centre of the campsite.

'This area is clear of trees and bushes. I think it's the best place to stage the attack.'

'Tina and Mike will be here.' He pointed to the very centre of the clearing. 'All the lights will be pointing on this area so we can see everything that is going on.'

'Graham and Lilly Anne will be positioned over here.' He pointed to the edge of the clearing. 'Bertha here, Juliet here and I will take up the last perimeter edge here.'

'Looks like you have all areas covered,' Mike said as he studied the map and the plans.

'Hopefully,' Graham said. 'We just have to make sure that we don't let the demon out of the clearing. If we do then there will be little hope of catching it if it reaches the trees.'

'Mike, can I ask you a question?' Bertha asked.

'Of course you can,' Mike replied between mouthfuls of sandwich.

'Do you think Tina loves you?'

Surprised by the question, Mike put down his plate and stared at Bertha. The quizzical look on his face made it clear that he wasn't sure where her line of questioning was going.

'Of course she does.'

'Do you think you would believe her if she said she didn't love you?'

Mike shrugged his shoulders. 'I don't know. I've never ever thought about it before. As far as I'm concerned I think we will always be together.'

'Just as I thought,' Bertha said half to herself. She looked slightly concerned.

'What's wrong, Bertha?' Lilly Anne asked.

'We may have a problem.'

'Why?' David asked.

'We need the demon to believe that Mike is upset that Tina hasn't reciprocated his love. How can Mike do that if he knows that she does love him?'

'Oh no,' Graham groaned. 'Bertha is right. Mike and Tina are just going to be acting. They really do love each other. It's not going to work. The demon won't come.'

'Why didn't we think of this before?' David added. He was annoyed. He had spent a long time working on the plan. He thought it was foolproof. Now all his hard work had been for nothing.

'That's just great,' Graham groaned again, getting to his feet. 'Are you telling me that we went after that thing for no reason? That David was tortured for nothing and that we didn't have to see those terrible things, the mutilated animal carcasses and the finger?'

‘What finger?’ Juliet asked. ‘Are you telling me that you found a body in Death Valley?’

Graham realised he had said too much seconds after the words had escaped from his mouth.

‘I thought we weren’t going to mention what we found at the cave,’ David said to Graham, his tone tense.

‘You can’t not tell us now,’ Mike interrupted. ‘I want to know what really happened.’

‘Does it matter now?’ Graham sighed. ‘It’s not as if we are going to be going up against the demon now.’

‘There still may be a way,’ Bertha said, half to herself. Her ebony brow crinkled with thought lines. ‘We know that Tina and Mike love each other but what we need is the demon to believe that Tina no longer has any affection for Mike.’

‘And how do we do that?’ Graham asked sarcastically.

‘We can’t do anything.’ Bertha turned to look at Mike. ‘It’s all up to you.’

‘Me?’ Mike gulped. ‘What do you want me to do? I hope you don’t want me and Tina to break up because that isn’t going to happen.’

‘Oh no.’ Bertha smiled. ‘On the night, when you tell Tina that you love her and she doesn’t respond, I want you to think about what it would feel like if she really didn’t love you anymore.’

‘I get you.’ Lilly Anne smiled at Bertha. ‘You want him to induce the feelings of loss, of total heartbreak.’

Bertha returned the smile. ‘Exactly.’ She turned her attention back to Mike. ‘It won’t be easy and it’s something that you cannot practise or the demon may seek you out at the wrong time.’

‘So I’ve got one shot at tricking the demon.’

‘Yes, Mike, you’ll only have one chance,’ Bertha confirmed. ‘Do you think you can do it?’

All eyes were now on Mike. They needed his full support, full commitment, otherwise they would have to call it off, the demon would be free to continue feeding on innocent, heartbroken people and there would be nothing they could do about it.

Mike finally grinned, a cheeky, cocky grin. ‘Yeah I’ll do it,’ he said turning his attention to Graham and David. ‘On one condition.’

‘Name it,’ Graham said, pleased that they were back on track.

‘Tell us about the finger.’

CHAPTER TWENTY-FIVE

It was now or never, Lilly Anne thought as Graham helped her into his car. She was dressed in navy dungarees, navy T-shirt and sensible, flat shoes. She was carrying a thick, padded jacket and a woolly hat. David had told her that it would be chilly at night and with heavy rain forecast, everyone should be dressed appropriately.

Bertha was already seated in the back of the car with Juliet. Likewise the two ladies were dressed warmly, also in dark colours as David had instructed. Both wore dark grey sweatpants and matching tops, walking boots and waterproof jackets.

Graham shut Lilly Anne's door before getting into the car himself. Under his coat he wore a Death Valley ranger's uniform, one of the two that David had somehow acquired. Once they reached the campsite he would remove his jacket and with David, they would secure the camp, making sure that no campers or visitors could access the site.

'Ready, ladies?' Graham chirped. He was trying to keep the mood light. He could see the nervousness in their faces and was already worried about Lilly Anne.

'Let's go,' Bertha said cheerfully, beaming her warm smile that could light up the darkest moment.

Graham honked the horn and David, who was driving the vehicle in front of them, waved before setting off down the driveway. Tina was sitting in the back of David's jeep with Mike. She turned to look at Lilly Anne, her face fraught with worry. She looked terrified.

Lilly Anne tried to smile but found it more difficult than she thought it would be. Everyone's emotions were overwrought. Nobody knew what was going to happen. What they were about to do was so dangerous, so crazy that Lilly Anne didn't want to think about it anymore or she knew she would tell Graham to stop the car so that she could get out.

The journey was much shorter than Lilly Anne had expected but as bumpy as she thought it would be. Her butt was sore and her back ached. The road up to the campsite hadn't been designed with pregnant women in mind.

Graham slowly brought the car to a stop in the middle of the clearing to let the ladies out before he parked the car some distance away, in a safer location. He pointed the car towards the road, left the car unlocked and the keys in the ignition, just in case they needed a quick getaway. David followed suit and then the pair joined the rest of the group.

A tall, lush juniper and pine-scented forest surrounded the picturesque campsite. To the side of the camp clearing, three tents had already been set up, three camouflage green, army issue tents. A small fire had been set up, but not lit and a kettle and pot were sitting on a log. Seven folding chairs had been set up in a ring around the fire and a large canister of water, full to the brim, was positioned just on the edge of the camp.

David and Graham had thought of everything, Lilly Anne smiled as she had a peep inside one of the tents. They had even laid out sleeping bags, utensils and toilet paper.

'This place is beautiful,' Lilly Anne said. She found it hard to believe that one of the most inhospitable places on the earth could be home to so many beautiful and unusual plants, flowers and trees.

David looked around, soaking up the idyllic scenery. He loved the great outdoors. 'Isn't it just.' he smiled.

'Where are the restrooms?' Juliet asked, looking around for a hut or cabin.

'This is the highest campsite on Telescope Peak,' David informed her. 'Up here you are at one with nature.' He grinned, knowing that Juliet was disgusted at the thought of doing her business out in the open. 'There are toilet pits over there.'

'Yuck,' Tina said and twisted her face. She was appalled too. 'I didn't sign up for that.'

'It's only for a few hours,' David said as he walked away from the two women. 'I'm sure you can handle a few hours of being up close and personal with Mother Nature.'

'We have decided to take rest breaks in shifts,' Graham informed them all. 'Two will have a break, two will watch for unwanted visitors and two will watch the camp.'

'There are seven of us,' Bertha put in.

'Lilly Anne is exempt from any of the duties and can take a break any time she wishes.'

'But…' Lilly Anne started to object but Graham was going to have none of it.

Graham put up a hand to stop her.

The determined look on his face told her that it would be stupid to argue with him.

'Okay,' she conceded.

'Tina and Mike, you two will be on campsite guard duty for the next two hours while Graham and I watch the road and surrounding area,' David instructed as he passed out the duties. He turned to Bertha and Juliet. 'You two better get some rest as you are going to be on campsite duty next.'

Juliet clicked her heels together and saluted. 'Yes, sir!'

Bertha, Lilly Anne and Mike giggled. They couldn't help it.

'Whoever is on guard must be vigilant at all times. We aren't just keeping an eye out for rangers and campers. We know the demon could be here. It could be watching us right now,' David said gravely, his voice sombre as he brought the hilarity to a swift stop. 'Whoever is on guard is responsible for the others' safety.'

'What do we do if the demon comes into camp?' Tina asked, looking around. The worried expression she wore earlier had again returned to her face.

David had four two-way radios. 'They are all set to frequency two.' He handed one to Mike, Bertha and Lilly Anne. 'If anything happens or if anyone sees someone or something, you must let the rest of us know.'

David looked around the huddled group. 'Okay?'

'Okay,' they all replied.

'Let's go, Graham,' David said as he attached the final radio to his belt.

'You go on,' Graham said to David. 'I'll be along in a minute.'

Everyone else started to head back to camp, except for Lilly Anne. She knew Graham wanted a moment alone with her.

'I hope you aren't going to tell me off for being overprotective,' he joked, once they were alone.

'No. I know you are right. I just don't want everyone to feel as if they have the added burden of looking after me.'

'Nobody is thinking like that.'

'I hope not.'

'We are all glad you came with us.' Graham smiled. 'Especially me.'

Lilly Anne's face turned pink. She felt like a giddy schoolgirl around him. He could turn her legs to jelly with smallest gesture of affection.

'How long do you expect to be keeping watch?' Lilly Anne asked.

'Until nightfall,' Graham said. 'That's when the valley floor goes quiet. Most of the visitors head back to Las Vegas around supper time, so we should be able to get the show on the road about nine.'

'Will I see you before then?'

'I hope so,' Graham answered. 'I was hoping that you would bring us some refreshments during the day.'

'Just let me know when you need something,' Lilly Anne said. It was good to feel needed. Finally she had something to do and she knew that Graham wanted her to feel like an important part of the team instead of the weak link.

'I'll see you later then.' Lilly Anne smiled and started to head back to camp.

'Lilly Anne,' Graham shouted. 'I need something before you go.'

Turning round Lilly Anne walked back to where Graham was standing. There was an amorous look in his eyes and he smiled coyly at her as she walked back to him.

'What do you need?' she spoke softly, bringing her eyes up to look at his handsome face. Her heart was pounding loudly and her senses and nerve endings were tingling with desire.

'A kiss,' Graham whispered as he lowered his head towards her. 'Just a kiss.'

As their lips locked, Lilly Anne and Graham forgot about the world around them. The demon, the quest and their inner fears vanished from their minds. This was their moment, their time and nothing was going to spoil it. Or so they thought.

CHAPTER TWENTY-SIX

'Lilly Anne, is Graham still with you?' David's voice sounded crackly as he spoke into the radio. 'If he is I need him now!' His voice was brisk. He sounded agitated.

Graham released Lilly Anne and took the radio from her.

'I'm on my way,' he spoke before handing the radio back to her. Taking to his heels he didn't even turn back to say goodbye. He knew that there was a problem and he hoped that David hadn't come across the demon, or vice versa, and that David was in danger again.

It took him about two minutes to reach David. He was standing at the side of the road. He had binoculars up to his eyes and he was watching something further down the dirt track.

'I'm here,' Graham puffed as he came alongside David. 'What you looking at?'

'A car,' David said, the binoculars still at his eyes. 'Full of teenagers by the looks of things.'

'Great,' Graham groaned. He had hoped that they wouldn't meet anyone. 'What do we do?' he asked as he heard the car engine. The car was getting closer.

'Leave the talking to me,' David said as he finally took the binoculars from his eyes and put on the grey, green ranger's cap that matched the immaculate ranger's uniform he wore.

Graham likewise put his hat on and tried to look and feel like a real ranger instead of the fraud he felt.

The car slowly rumbled up the hill towards them, winding through the narrow track. By the sound of things the stereo volume had been turned up as far as it could go and loud, guitar music was blasting through the speakers and open windows, shattering the peaceful, idyllic, tranquillity of the valley.

David walked into the middle of the road and stood there, waiting for the car to reach them. As the vehicle neared, he raised his hand and motioned to the driver to stop.

When the car finally came to a halt, three male teenagers jumped out and walked up to David. They were all dressed in T-shirts and baggy jeans, their hair unkempt and shoulder length and two of them had a nose piercing. They were laughing and whispering.

'Is there a problem?' the blonde-haired one asked cockily.

'The camp is closed for the night,' David informed them, his voice curt. He didn't like the little punks.

'You are kidding, man,' one of the two dark-haired boys said, looking annoyed. 'Why's the camp shut?'

The other dark-haired boy was smoking a cigarette. He took a long drag before flicking the still-lit butt on to the dusty road.

'Pick that up,' David commanded. He could feel his temper rising. They obviously had no respect for the beautiful surroundings or the wildlife that thrived in the valley.

'What's your problem, old man?' the dark-haired youth asked as he bent down and picked up the butt. 'You need to chill out.'

Graham could see that David was ready to snap. He could see him grabbing hold of the boy and beating the crap out of him until he learnt to show respect for his elders.

'The camp is closed to tourists for tonight only. A party of geology students have booked the site for the night. It will be open again tomorrow.'

'So where do we go tonight?' the blonde youth asked.

'Turn back and go back to the valley floor,' David stepped in. 'Drive about a mile and a half into the valley and there will be a sign for another campsite.'

'Thanks, man,' one of the dark-haired boys said as they all turned and headed back to the car.

'Hey,' David shouted after them. 'We'll be keeping an eye on you three,' he informed them. 'I don't want to catch any of you throwing away lit cigarettes or starting fires unless they are in the designated areas. Understand?'

'Yes, sir,' the blonde youth replied. He looked annoyed at being told off and pushed the dark-haired boy that had stupidly thrown away the lit cigarette to let him know that his stupid behaviour may have ruined their trip.

Graham and David watched as the car turned and drove back down the dirt track and headed along the road that divided the dry, arid, desert floor of the valley. They watched it until it disappeared from view before taking off their hats.

'Little shits,' David said to Graham.

'You were once that age,' Graham joked, trying to calm David down.

'Yeah, but I was never that disrespectful.'

'Things have changed,' Graham said as they walked further up the road. 'Kids no longer seem to be taught the same values and principles we were.'

'My girls are,' David informed him as they reached the end of the road that led to the entrance of the camp. 'They would never speak to a grown-up the way those boys spoke to us.'

'Speaking of your kids,' Graham said. 'Where do your kids and wife think you are?'

'Here.'

'Really?' Graham was surprised.

'I told them I was going on a camping trip for a few days with some old air force buddies.'

'Your wife didn't mind?'

'No, not at all, she's used to my spur-of-the-moment trips,' David said looking up at the grey sky as he held a hand out. 'Looks like the weatherman was right.'

Moments later the heavens seemed to open and heavy rain started to fall from the sky. Dark spots started to appear on their uniforms and David and Graham picked up their pace.

'Where are we going?' Graham asked David as they peeled off to the right and into the forest.

'I found a birdwatching hut,' David told him. 'We can shelter in there.'

'What about the road?'

'We can still see it.'

A few moments later they were at the small, brown hut. David opened the door and let Graham in before getting in and closing the door. It was dark and a bit smelly. The only light came from the small, slatted windows.

Graham took a seat on one of the folding chairs that David had already set up and stared out of the small gap. David had been right, not only could they see the road, they could see the valley floor.

'Here,' David said and handed Graham a beer.

'Cheers,' Graham said taking the can from David. He certainly was full of surprises.

'You had better savour it,' David told him. 'I only brought the two.'

'Then I suggest we make a toast,' Graham said. 'Here's to new friendships.'

David smiled. 'I'll drink to that.' He rapped his can against Graham's before taking a hearty drink.

'David and Graham,' a voice crackled.

David took the radio from his belt. 'What can we do for you, Lilly Anne?'

'I'm just checking in. Thought you would like to know that all is well here and there have been no unwanted visitors,' she informed them. 'How are you two getting on? Have you managed to get out of the rain?'

'Yeah,' David said. 'We are fine and holed up in a birdwatcher's hut. We are going to stay here for a while.'

'Okay. Let me know if you need anything.'

Lilly Anne switched off the radio and set it down on the cot beside her. She would have liked to speak to Graham.

The rain was coming down hard and it made a tapping noise as it came into contact with the tent.

'Anyone home?' Juliet said as she opened the tent doorway. Her jacket was fastened right up and the hood came down and covered half of her face.

'I thought you might like some company.' she smiled as she quickly secured the tent again to stop the rain from soaking everything inside. She removed her wet jacket and laid it on one of the chairs that Lilly Anne had brought indoors when it had started raining.

'I thought you were bunking with Bertha.'

'I was until she started snoring,' Juliet said taking a seat on the cot opposite Lilly Anne. 'What a racket.'

Lilly Anne giggled. 'I know. I can sometimes hear her during the night.'

Juliet made herself more comfortable.

'How are you bearing up?'

'I'm okay.' Lilly Anne sighed. 'Being cooped up in here for the last few hours hasn't helped and this isn't the most comfortable of beds.'

'Hopefully the rain will ease off soon.'

'I hope so. It's starting to get dark. I want to get this evening over with.'

'Are you scared?' Juliet asked.

'Yes. Of course I am.'

Juliet exhaled deeply. 'So am I. I can't stop thinking about what could happen if this goes wrong.'

'How are the others?' Lilly Anne asked. 'Have you spoken to Tina or Mike?'

'I popped my head into their tent before I came in here,' she informed her. 'Tina looks scared out of her wits. Mike and her are all cuddled up. It would have looked romantic if she wasn't holding on so tightly. I think she is terrified to let him go.'

'It must be hard for her,' Lilly Anne confessed sadly. 'That poor girl has to watch her boyfriend being taken over by the demon and no matter what we all hope and think, we have no real idea of what the demon will do to him.'

'Let's stop talking about it,' Juliet said, closing her eyes and lying back on the small bed. 'Let's talk about something more positive.'

'Like what?'

Juliet opened her eyes and turned to look at Lilly Anne. ‘Like what’s going on with you and Graham.’

Lilly Anne blushed bright red.

‘I saw you kissing.’

‘So?’ Lilly Anne giggled.

‘Was it nice?’ Juliet asked propping herself up. ‘Was it the first time or have you kissed him before?’

‘Yes it was very nice and no it was not our first proper kiss.’

Juliet grinned. She was so pleased for them. ‘At least something good has come out of this.’

CHAPTER TWENTY-SEVEN

After what felt like an eternity to Graham, the sun finally began to fade and as darkness started to descend on the valley, David decided it was time to head back to the camp.

'Thank goodness,' Graham said getting out of the cramped hut.

The rain had finally stopped and it was time to get the show on the road. As they walked towards camp, the four lights that David had brought were fired up. Mike was getting things ready.

As they neared the lit-up area, they could make out Tina and Bertha. They were getting the weapons ready, completing the tasks that David had given them. Mike was busy checking the lights and Juliet was putting the fire out.

Lilly Anne emerged from the tent as they reached camp.

'Hi there.' She smiled, pleased to see the two men and glad that neither of them had been harmed.

Graham walked up to her. 'How have you been?'

'Fine.' She smiled but this time it looked strained.

'Are you still sure you want to be here?' Graham asked.

'Yes. I need to be here.'

Bertha handed her the knife that David had allocated to her. 'Can you come and join us?' she asked.

Lilly Anne and Graham followed her to where the others were standing.

‘I would like to say something before we begin,’ she said. ‘I know that most of you aren’t religious but I would like to say a prayer if you will allow me.’

Nobody objected. Instead most of them bowed their heads in respect as Bertha began.

‘Dear God, I come before you to ask, no plead, for your protection. What we are about to do is very dangerous but we all know the risks involved and know that we have to destroy the demon if any of us are to live with peace of mind. We are doing it for Lilly Anne’s unborn baby and for little Lennox, so they can always be safe. We are also doing it for Patrick and for all who have been slain by the evil creature. May they all rest in peace.’

Graham reached out and took hold of Lilly Anne’s hand. He squeezed it gently. He hoped that if God existed that he was listening and that he would give them the protection they so needed.

‘Please God, grant us your favour and let us be triumphant tonight. Amen.’

‘Amen,’ echoed around the group.

Nobody moved for a few moments. They stood there in the huddle, fear and worry strained across their faces.

‘Let’s do it,’ David finally said.

Mike and Tina walked to the centre of the lit area as Juliet, Bertha and David took up their positions. Graham led Lilly Anne over to his designated area and they stood beneath one of the lights.

‘I don’t want you leaving my side,’ he whispered to her.

‘I don’t intend to,’ she whispered back.

‘Okay, Tina and Mike, it’s up to you!’ David shouted from the opposite side of the lit area. ‘Whenever you are ready!’

Tina kissed Mike on the cheek and hugged him tightly. Then she took a few steps back. Mike took a deep breath. 'I love you, Tina.'

There was silence, an eerie, unpleasant silence. Lilly Anne looked around her for signs that the demon was near but didn't see or hear anything. She wondered if Mike had managed to convince the demon that he was heartbroken.

Mike stared at Tina. He looked into her wet eyes. She was about to start crying and he used her sadness to make himself imagine how upset, how heartbroken he would be if she really didn't love him. He imagined her with another guy. One of his friends and he didn't like the thought of someone else touching her, someone else arousing her. He didn't like the feeling of loss or the ache in his heart at the idea of Tina loving someone else.

Trying to concentrate, he didn't notice the look on Tina's face changing. Before she had looked upset and worried, now she was terrified. Her eyes were following something moving on the edge of the forest.

'Look!' Graham whispered as the hairs on the back of his neck stood on end. 'It's here.'

Lilly Anne caught sight of the demon. A grey-black shadow hovering by the trees, watching and waiting for the right moment to attack Mike.

'He's doing it,' she whispered. 'It believes he is heartbroken,' she said as the demon began to move towards Mike and Tina.

Tina closed her eyes as she tried to control her overwrought emotions. Her breathing became deep and erratic and she was sure she was about to suffer a panic attack. She opened her eyes again just as the demon moved alongside Mike. The shadowy figure hugged the grassy land as it slithered towards him. Mike still hadn't noticed the demon. He was still concentrating. Still trying to make the demon believe that he was heartbroken.

Tina covered her mouth with her hand as she tried to stifle a scream as the smoky figure started to rise from the ground. She couldn't do it. She couldn't stand by and watch it take Mike. She loved him too much.

'I love you!' she yelled at the top of her voice. 'Get away from him you bastard!' she continued to shout. 'I love him!'

'No!' Mike shouted as the shadowy figure instantly reacted to Tina's words. It recoiled, as if Tina's words of love had injured it.

'Oh no,' David groaned as he started to run towards Tina and Mike. 'Get the hell out of there!'

After a few seconds the demon seemed to have regained composure. The swirling, black mass of pure evil doubled in size and towered over the cowering couple.

'He's mine,' it hissed. It sounded angry and it hovered in front of Tina and Mike and when they tried to pass it or run around it, it moved in front of them again.

'Help us!' Tina screamed as she held on to Mike. She was petrified. What had she done, she should never have agreed to the plan in the first place. Now she had put everyone in danger.

'Get away from them!' Graham shouted as he also ran towards the frightened couple.

The demon recognised his voice. 'You!' it hissed and started to move towards Graham.

'Oh no,' he said, reeling on his heels as he tried to run. His feet slipped on the wet grass and he fell on his butt.

'Leave him alone!' Lilly Anne shouted at the demon. Instantly realising that she shouldn't have.

The shadowy figure moved right past Graham. 'Hello, Lilly Anne,' it hissed.

The light above Lilly Anne's head exploded in a brilliant, bright flash. Hot glass rained down on her head and she tried to protect herself with her hands. Hot, sharp shards cut into her hands and the top of her head as she fell to the ground in a crumpled heap.

The demon started to laugh. A blood-curdling laugh that made the hairs on the back of Graham's neck stand on end. Getting to his feet he ran to where Lilly Anne was lying. Her hands were bleeding and a trickle of blood ran down her forehead.

'Oh no,' she groaned as she clutched her stomach with her bloody hands. 'The baby, it's coming.'

'Not now,' Graham said. 'It can't be!'

'It is,' Lilly Anne groaned again. 'I'm scared, Graham.'

'It will be all right,' Graham said as he helped her lean against a tree stump as the demon continued to wreak havoc on the rest of the group.

Bertha and Juliet were screaming. Mike was trying to console Tina and David looked as if he didn't know what to do.

Lilly Anne moaned, as the contractions got stronger. She grabbed hold of Graham's hand. 'Please help me get out of here. I don't want the demon getting hold of my baby. Please don't let my son die.'

'I won't let the demon hurt you or the baby,' he said in a soothing voice as he tried to calm her down. He was really worried about her and was concerned for the welfare of the baby. 'The demon won't get anywhere near the baby. I love you, Lilly Anne, and I will protect you and the baby with my life if I have to.'

‘You love me?’ Lilly Anne said. She looked stunned at Graham’s revelation.

‘Yes I do. I love you with all my heart.’

Lilly Anne was speechless. She didn’t know how to react. She was having her baby, James’s baby and it just didn’t seem right for them to be discussing their feelings at a time when James was so prominently in her thoughts.

The sadness was unmistakable in Graham’s eyes as he got to his feet. She didn’t love him. He was sure of it. If she had been in love with him, surely she would have told him. So consumed by his grief, that he was trying to hide from her, he didn’t notice the demon. It had stopped attacking the others. It was homing in on him. It had felt his heart break.

The demon entered Graham’s body as Lilly Anne watched on in horror. David rushed over to where Lilly Anne lay.

‘What happened?’ David asked her as he watched Graham’s body turn limp.

‘He told me he loved me,’ she wept.

‘Do you love him?’ David asked her as he continued to watch Graham. He knew the demon had begun to consume his friend’s soul.

‘Do you love him?’ he shouted at Lilly Anne. ‘Because if you do, you had better let him know before it is too late.’

Of course she loved him and as she watched him standing before her in a comatose state she was reminded of James and how he had been taken from her. If she had expressed her love to him, he wouldn’t have died in such a horrible way and now if she didn’t let Graham know how she felt soon, she would lose him too.

‘I love you, Graham!’ she yelled at the top of her voice.

Graham’s body went stiff instantly as the demon responded to her voice.

'I love you, Graham!' she shouted again.

Graham's body started to shake and twitch. He fell to the ground, his body hitting the grass hard as he continued to shudder uncontrollably. He looked like he was having a seizure.

'It's killing him,' Lilly Anne cried. She was sure she had left it too long and now Graham would die at the hands of the demon just as her husband had.

Bertha and the others had gathered around Graham.

'What do we do?' Juliet asked concerned. 'How do we help him?'

'Get out of him you, bastard!' Bertha shouted and rapped Graham across his legs with the baseball bat. 'Get out! Get out!' she continued to shout as she hit him again.

David pulled the bat from her hands, as she was about to swing it again.

'What the hell are you doing?' he asked totally in awe, annoyed with Bertha's oddball behaviour.

'I'm sorry,' Bertha sniffed. 'I just can't stand by and watch the demon take him. We need to help him.'

'But I don't think hitting him is the right thing to do,' David said sarcastically before kneeling down beside Lilly Anne.

She was in a lot of pain, clutching her heavily pregnant abdomen. 'Tell him again,' he instructed her. 'Tell him again how you feel. He's obviously fighting the demon but he needs help and I think you are the only person who can help him right now.'

Lilly Anne stared at Graham as he writhed and wriggled on the ground. Was he still able to hear her? Or had she been too late? Had his soul already been consumed by the demon?

'I love you, Graham!' she shouted again as Juliet knelt down at the other side of her and wiped away the trickle of blood on her forehead with a clean, white handkerchief that she had taken from her jacket pocket.

'Don't leave me, Graham! I love you and need you!'

Graham started to bang his head on the ground as two more of the lights exploded.

Bertha and Tina screamed and cowered as Mike held on to them protectively as they were plunged into near darkness as the wind started to get up. One of the tents was blown over and tumbled away into the trees, the contents spilling out with every roll.

'This isn't good,' David said more to himself than anyone else as he looked around. Something was about to happen, something big and he had a nasty feeling that nobody was prepared for it. He had to find a safe place for Lilly Anne. 'Help me with Lilly Anne,' he ordered Juliet.

Juliet and David helped Lilly Anne to her feet and struggled to get her out of harm's way. The wind had quickened and they fought to stay on their feet as they desperately tried to reach the edge of the forest. As they neared the trees David selected a thick, bushy area that would shade Lilly Anne from the wind and keep her hidden.

'Stay with her,' David told Juliet and handed her his torch. 'Whatever happens don't come back to the camp. You have to keep Lilly Anne and the baby safe.'

'Okay,' Juliet replied looking frightened.

David got to his feet and started to head back to the clearing.

'David!' Juliet shouted after him. 'I'll be back in a moment,' she told Lilly Anne before running after David.

'What is it?' he asked her.

'What if she can't hold on?' Juliet said breathlessly. 'I don't know how to deliver a baby.'

David took hold of Juliet's shoulders. 'I know that and I know that I am expecting a lot from you but I need you to be strong for Lilly Anne's sake. I think the demon is about to come out of Graham's body and if it does and we don't deal with it before it finds Lilly Anne, I hate to think what it will do to her.'

'You think it will want revenge!' Juliet's eyes were wide with worry, the whites nearly fully exposed. She looked petrified.

David nodded grimly. 'She stopped it.'

CHAPTER TWENTY-EIGHT

'How is he?' David asked Mike as he reached the others.

'I don't know,' Mike said. He was kneeling down beside Graham. 'He stopped fitting a few minutes ago.'

David looked down at Graham. He was very pale and his body was contorted, one arm outstretched about his head, the other stretched out to the side and his legs were entwined together. He was moaning and groaning, his face twisted with pain.

'I hope I didn't damage him,' Bertha said nervously, the wind was billowing round them and they were huddled together for protection from the furious gale.

David leaned down towards Graham. 'Can you hear me, Graham?' he shouted, trying to be heard over the loud whistling sound of the wind.

'I don't think he is conscious!' Mike shouted loudly so he could be heard, but it wasn't needed. Just as the wind had suddenly started, it came to a dramatic stop.

David looked around, the hairs on the back of his neck were standing on end and he was sweating with nervous expectation. The quiet was as deafening as the howling wind. There was something strange and wrong about the eerie silence.

'Get your weapons ready,' David commanded, getting his gun prepared.

Tina looked at Mike. She was tearful. 'This is my fault. Graham could die because of me.'

Mike didn't reply. He didn't know what to say. Part of him felt guilty for the relief he felt at Tina chickening out and saving him from Graham's fate. The other part of him felt sorry and worried for Graham. Was he going to survive the night? Were any of them going to survive the night?

'Look!' Bertha shouted. 'Graham is awake.'

Graham's eyes had opened but he didn't seem to be fully conscious. He stared straight up at the starry sky as if he was mesmerised by the bright, twinkling lights.

'Graham?' David leaned in closer. He turned to look at the others. 'I think we need to get him to a hospital.'

Before anyone could respond Graham grabbed David by the throat. His movement was fast, his grip tight and he crushed his fingers forcefully around David's vocal cords. David pulled at Graham's hand but to no avail, he was so strong, so powerful, the demon was controlling him.

Graham thrust David aside and got to his feet.

'Shit! What do we do!' Mike was panicking as Graham moved towards him. He didn't want to hurt him. He saw Graham's gun lying on the ground and he scrambled to get to it. Reaching it he cocked it before turning it on Graham.

'Stay away!' he shouted. 'Or I'll shoot!'

'Don't!' David shouted as he rushed Graham, tackling him from behind, taking him off guard and hurling him to the ground.

Graham didn't put up a fight. He groaned and moaned and then his body went rigid again.

David let him go and got to his feet again as Graham started to fit. This time it was worse than before, every part of his body was shaking uncontrollably, his eyes had rolled into the back of his head and he was drooling. He opened his mouth and his stomach started to retch as if he were about to be sick.

Bertha linked her hands together, raised her eyes to the sky and started to pray loudly.

'I think it's a bit late for that,' Mike said sarcastically. He didn't believe in God before tonight and after seeing Graham suffer so, he was sure that no loving creator could exist, or why would they stand by and watch a good man suffer and die at the hands of something so evil and ungodly?

What looked like gas or smoke started to pour from Graham's mouth. Black, billowing smoke, swirling in a circular motion.

'Here we go,' David said and cocked his gun. 'Get ready everyone,' he ordered as Graham's mouth closed. 'Tina, check Graham. Make sure he is breathing.'

David gave his orders as he watched the smoky cloud begin to change into something more solid. A shape started to form in the middle of the black, hazy cloud, a very tall, broad and powerful figure that had to be at least seven foot in height.

'Jesus,' he muttered under his breath. It was huge.

The demon continued to change into its true form. The transformation was quick and before anyone had time to run, the demon stood before them, a big, hulking, hell beast of brown fur, horns, talons and teeth.

Three big horns ran down the centre of the demon's head, the middle one the longest of the three and probably used for skewering victims. Its overlarge hands or paws were finished by evil-looking, long, sharp nails that would slice through flesh and bone easily. Now it had not just the capability of stealing their souls, it could rip them apart limb from limb.

As it continued to solidify, it homed in on David. Breathing deeply, plumes of steaming hot breath billowed from its broad nose and wide nostrils. Its lifeless, hollow eyes burned into David like hot, burning coals. It wanted him dead and it showed him its powerful jaws and razor-sharp teeth, growling as it did so, the deep, throaty sound chilling David to the bone.

Mike was the first to react. Somehow he managed to pull himself out of the hypnotic trance that seemed to have the others fixed to the spot. Raising his gun, he fired off three shots in the direction of the demon.

To David it was like slow motion, as if time was about to stand still. He watched in intense expectation as the bullets whizzed past him and hit the creature. Each was a direct hit on the beast's abdomen. There were three loud popping sounds followed by three dull thumps as the demon squealed and reeled back in pain as bright green goo oozed from the bullet wounds.

Then all hell broke loose. The demon screamed again. The bellowing, chilling scream echoed all around them, and no doubt woke all the living creatures that inhabited Death Valley.

The demon surged forward as Mike fired the remaining three shots. They had also been aimed perfectly and hit the creature's huge, powerful chest. The same disgusting green goo splattered out of the wounds.

'I'm out!' Mike shouted at David and turned to run as the demon lunged at him. It had been Graham's gun and he had the extra bullets.

Before Mike could successfully get out of the demon's path, it reached out and grabbed him by the left arm. Mike squealed in pain and tried desperately to break free from the powerful grip.

'Help me!' he yelled as the demon bared its teeth and squeezed harder. There was a loud snapping noise and Mike yelled loudly, his face scrunched up in pain. The demon had crushed his arm, snapping the bones like dry twigs.

David fired two shots. The first hit the demon in the right shoulder. The second skimmed the fleshy area of the neck, gouging out a large chunk of hair-covered flesh.

The demon released Mike and turned to look at David. It was now mad with rage and it ran at him at full speed, barely giving David enough time to squeeze off three more rounds.

Three bullets hit the demon in the chest, but it continued unthwarted as it charged towards David. David squeezed the trigger again and the last bullet hit the demon square between the eyes, stopping it dead in its tracks.

David quickly reloaded his gun as the demon swayed and swaggered about as if it was drunk. Tina and Bertha rushed forward courageously, Bertha wielding her baseball bat, Tina armed with the hunting knife.

Tina reached the demon first and with a powerful thrust, rammed the blade into the back of the demon's right leg, just above the knee. It wobbled uneasily and then the leg gave way and it fell to its knees. Screaming like a banshee, Bertha rushed towards it, gripping her bat tightly with both hands, she launched a series of hard blows to the top of the demon's head.

'Get away from it, Bertha!' David shouted as he pointed the reloaded gun at the demon.

Bertha turned on her heels to run but her hefty frame slowed her down and the demon lashed out at her, catching her on the back. It plunged its long, razor-sharp talons deep into her flesh. She spun round in pain and terror. The demon attacked again and in one swift, agile movement, it ripped open her throat, severing her jugular vein.

Instinctively Bertha put her hands up to her neck as she tried to slow the blood flow but inside she knew it was over and she turned to look at David.

David didn't know what to do. Panic engulfed his senses and he was glued to the spot, unable to move, unable to help poor Bertha. He watched as she tried to speak, but she could only make gurgling noises. He could hear Tina screaming. Screaming loudly and hysterically. Mike was swearing, shouting a lot of obscenities at the demon and he threw his gun at it. David still couldn't move and he watched the gun bounce off the side of the demon's head as a blood-soaked and dying Bertha fell to the ground in a crumpled heap.

Tina was still screaming, but David could hear another woman's voice. It was Juliet.

She had witnessed everything and she was screaming as loudly and as hysterically as Tina.

The demon had also heard Juliet and it turned to look for her. Its evil eyes skimming the edge of the forest until it caught sight of her.

Juliet instantly stopped screaming. She could see the demon getting up. It was coming for her. Instinctively she turned and fled into the forest.

'Lilly Anne,' David said mostly to himself and rushed after the demon, with his gun aimed.

'Help me up,' Graham said weakly, tugging on Mike's leg, giving the young man a fright.

'Jesus!' he yelled jumping back, before smiling. 'You're awake, man.'

'What happened?' Graham asked. His voice was hoarse and he was still very pale and weak.

'The demon took you over,' Mike told him, helping Graham to his feet.

'Where's Lilly Anne?' Graham said, panic in his voice, his eyes searching frantically for the woman he loved. He caught sight of Bertha, covered in blood and stone dead. Then he heard gunshots and Juliet screaming.

'Where's Lilly Anne?' he asked Mike again, frantically.

'In the forest.'

'The demon?'

'In the forest.'

'Where's my gun?'

Mike ran over to where it had landed. Graham followed on shaky legs. He opened the barrel and reloaded the gun. Then he ran towards the wood in search of the others.

'Get Tina out of here,' he instructed Mike. 'There is nothing more either of you can do now.'

Mike didn't have to be told twice and as Graham headed into the forest, he picked up Tina and the two of them ran in the opposite direction.

CHAPTER TWENTY-NINE

Juliet had removed Lilly Anne's dungarees and briefs. The baby was coming and Juliet had panicked when the top of the baby's head had appeared. She had run off to get help leaving Lilly Anne alone.

Leaning against a tree trunk, squatting, her legs wide open, her dignity an afterthought, Lilly Anne wondered if her unborn baby would survive the night.

She needed to push, but was too scared to do so when there was no one to help her. Hearing rustling in the bushes, she bit on her bottom lip, trying to stop herself from screaming with pain as another contraction gripped her abdomen and made her want to push even more.

Juliet appeared, running towards her as fast as her legs could carry her. She looked worried and scared.

'We have to go,' she said to Lilly Anne.

'What?' Lilly Anne replied. 'You are kidding me. I can't go anywhere. The baby is coming.'

'The demon,' Juliet said breathlessly, as she looked around behind her. 'It's coming this way.'

Lilly Anne didn't say anything. She didn't have to. Juliet could see the panic in her eyes.

There was more rustling close by and the two ladies jumped and clung on to one another.

'You have to help me hide,' Lilly Anne begged Juliet. 'Then you will have to lure it away from here.'

'I don't know if I can,' Juliet confessed tearfully. 'I'm too scared,' she sniffed as David appeared in the small clearing before them.

'David,' Lilly Anne cried out in relief.

'We have to get you out of here,' he said to Lilly Anne.

'It's too late,' she told David. 'The baby's head is crowning.' She groaned again loudly. The contractions were closer together and there was no way she could put off giving birth any longer.

'I've got to push,' she said to Juliet. 'The baby's coming.'

Juliet helped get Lilly Anne more comfortable. David stood guard, watching the bushes and trees around them for any sign of the demon.

Out of the corner of his eye David caught sight of a missile coming towards him, he ducked just in time to stop the large log from hitting him in the head. It bounced off the tree next to him. Splinters broke off and showered down on his head like little, sharp needles.

Another log hurtled towards him and he ducked down low, trying to keep out of the way of the barrage of missiles. Juliet and Lilly Anne were cowering in fear. David knew he would have to do something, Lilly Anne couldn't be moved and by the looks of things, the baby's head was nearly out.

Just as he stood up again, out of nowhere the demon appeared before him. It hit him in the face, knocking him from his feet. The gun flew out of his hand and he reeled backwards, his back and head hitting a tree hard. He fell to the ground unconscious.

The two women screamed as the demon moved towards them. It homed in on Lilly Anne and it grinned evilly, it wanted her baby. It wanted to kill her baby.

Juliet closed her eyes and protectively lay across Lilly Anne. She was the last line of defence. Not that it was much of a defence.

A dull popping sound made her open her eyes again and she turned to look at the demon. It had stopped dead and it appeared to be staring into space.

There was another pop, and then another, then the back of the demon's head seemed to explode. Bits of brain and spurts of green goo shot out in all directions, some of which landed on the two ladies.

The demon's eyes rolled into the back of its skull and it fell to its knees as another bullet entered the hole in the back of its head and exited out of its left cheek. Graham walked up to it and kicked it down on to the ground.

'Graham!' Lilly Anne cried out with joy.

Graham looked at her for a brief moment, smiled and then turned his attention back to the demon. It was still alive, barely, and its chest heaved uneasily with every laboured breath.

Taking more bullets from his pocket, he reloaded the gun, pointed it at the area of the chest where he hoped to find the heart and expelled five bullets.

The beast screamed loudly and writhed in pain for a few minutes. It looked up at Graham, its eyes glazed and there was a defeated look that pleased him.

'Go back to hell!' Graham shouted and then shot the last bullet into the gaping hole that had once been the demon's chest.

The demon screamed again, a loud, piercing scream that hurt Graham's ears. Juliet and Lilly Anne covered their ears as the ground around the demon began to shake.

Graham fell over and scrambled away from the demon's carcass as the ground beneath it began to open up. He crawled over to Lilly Anne and Juliet.

The ground around the demon continued to open. It was like a mini earthquake. The sound of the earth parting was deafening and bushes and shrubs started to slide into the ground as the demon's body disappeared into the crack that had appeared. Then the ground slowly closed up again and the demon was gone.

Lilly Anne groaned loudly as her son was born. Juliet wrapped the screaming baby in her coat and Graham cut the umbilical cord before handing James Junior to his mother.

There was a moan from David as Graham helped him sit up. 'Can you walk?'

'Yeah,' he said rubbing the back of his head and feeling a large lump. He was going to have a splitting headache later.

'You okay?' he asked Graham.

'Yeah, I'm fine and I'm a dad,' he grinned.

David smiled. 'How are baby and mom?'

'Just great but I need to get them to the hospital.'

Juliet gently took James from Lilly Anne. Graham helped David to his feet and the two men joined the ladies.

Graham gently picked Lilly Ann up and held her securely in his arms. She wasn't fit to walk, she had been through a lot in the last few hours.

'Where is Bertha?' Lilly Anne asked worriedly and seeing David and Graham's expressions she knew something was wrong.

'She didn't make it,' David told her.

A tear ran down Lilly Anne's cheek. Bertha had been the one that had brought them all together. She was the one that had found a way to kill the demon and free everyone from a life of fear and worry.

'I want to see her,' she whispered as the tears continued to spill from her wet eyes.

As they reached the edge of the trees, they noticed Mike and Tina. Mike's arm was in a sling and Tina was covering Bertha's body with a blanket.

'I thought I told you two to get out of here.' David smiled.

'We couldn't go without the rest of the team.' Mike grinned back. 'Looks like we have a new addition to the family.'

Tina walked up to Juliet and looked down at the bundle she was holding. 'He's beautiful.'

'Can I hold him?' Tina asked.

'Of course you can,' Lilly Anne said with a smile as she looked at the face of her new son. He was sleeping and looked so cosy and comfortable wrapped up in the coat.

As Tina was passed James, Graham carried Lilly Anne over to where Bertha lay and kneeled down so that Lilly Anne could see her friend.

Lilly Anne reached out and pulled back the blanket, just far enough to see Bertha's sweet face.

'Goodbye, old lady,' she said as tears streamed down her face. 'I'm going to miss you. We're all going to miss you.'

She replaced the blanket and Graham got back on his feet. He held Lilly Anne tight against him as she cried.

'Let's get you to the hospital,' Graham said making his way towards where the cars were parked.

'Mike and I will stay here until the police arrive,' David said. 'You take the ladies to the hospital.'

'What will you tell them?' Juliet asked.

'I don't know yet,' David confessed and looked at Mike. 'But I'm sure we will think of something.'

Graham led the ladies back to the car and helped Lilly Anne in before getting in himself. Tina passed James back to his mother.

Graham rubbed his sore thighs before starting the engine.

'It's over.' He sighed with relief, turning to look at Lilly Anne. 'We are safe now. Things can get back to normal.'

Lilly Anne looked down at her sleeping son. He would never know about tonight, never know about the danger he had been in. She smiled and gently ran a finger over his forehead.

She looked at Graham, her eyes full of love and admiration for the man that had saved her son. 'Come on, Daddy; let's get this little one to the hospital.'